WALK IN DEEP SHADOWS

Sara Mitchell

ACCENT BOOKS
Denver, Colorado

ACCENT BOOKS

A division of Accent Publications, Inc.
12100 West Sixth Avenue
P.O. Box 15337
Denver, Colorado 80215

Copyright © 1989 Sara Mitchell
Printed in the United States of America

Library of Congress Catalog Card Number 88-83752

ISBN 0-89636-252-3

Dedicated to
B.J. Hoff
an encourager, friend, and sister in Christ
who really believed I could do it!

Acknowledgments

With gratitude and appreciation to:
Dr. Richard A. Lawrence who cheerfully let me "borrow" his offices as the inspiration for the Prescott mansion.

Carol Hall who assisted me with musical references.

Sergeants Kean and Alumbaugh of the Colorado Springs Police Department for answering a multitude of questions.

PROLOGUE

In a room used to constant activity, the lack of motion was more alarming than a tornado siren.

The Space Operations Control Center at Falcon Air Force Station, Colorado, was a room dominated by computer systems and peripherals. These, in turn, dominated the lives of a handful of civilian and military personnel handpicked from all branches of the armed services. At this moment, however, the computers and the personnel were at a standstill.

Something was wrong. Very wrong.

A chilling, detached message was flashing on two of the computer screens as well as on the main system monitor:

SOFTWARE FATAL ERROR ENCOUNTERED
PROCESS ABORTED

The test director, a civilian contractor in charge of the operation, stared in grim disbelief at the message a half-minute longer before turning to an equally frozen Air Force colonel.

"I don't believe it," he said between clenched teeth. "It's happened again."

The colonel tore his gaze from the screens and reached for the nearest phone, punching out some all-too-familiar numbers. "This is Col. Sinclair. I need to talk to the Admiral."

Waiting tensely, he pressed two white knuckled fingers against the vein throbbing at his temple. "Admiral Vale, this is Joe." He listened a moment, his mouth tightening. "No, sir. It just crashed again."

After a longer pause during which the lines scoring his face deepened and wintry blue eyes chilled even further, he replaced the receiver and looked around the room. He knew this particular room better than the living room of his home, and for the past twenty-seven months probably had spoken to the staff more than he had his wife and three kids. The culmination of twenty-one years of backbreaking work and unquenchable dreams was bound up in one thirty-by-forty foot room.

But now a lifetime of work teetered on the edge of despair because a highly sophisticated blinking bucket of bolts continued to announce with total indifference:

SOFTWARE FATAL ERROR ENCOUNTERED
PROCESS ABORTED

Process aborted. . .two hundred and fifty million dollars wiped out.

Process aborted. . .and the future safety of the United States of America rested on perilously shaky ground.

More than a dozen people were sitting and standing in the room, each staring at him from their computer consoles. A couple of the civilian technicians were still frantically pushing buttons and keys; SMSgt. Greco gestured angrily as he spoke to someone on the phone. Everyone else remained in suspended animation, waiting for someone to tell them what to do.

Still silent and uncaring, the message flashed away on two screens and the main system monitor.

Col. Sinclair turned to Archie, the test director. "We'd better get over to the base. Admiral Vale is waiting."

Twenty minutes later they entered Admiral Vale's office. The admiral was pacing angrily back and forth across the navy blue carpet in front of his desk. "This was *supposed* to be a breakthrough in weapons tracking technology. We promised the Secretary some solid results before Congress adjourns for this fiscal year." He divided a flinty look between the two men who had just entered. "That room you just left is the heart of the most significant defense program since the building of the Ark. What's the

6

hang-up now? I want answers—and I want results, gentlemen."

Archie Cohen sat slumped in a chair, his hands worrying the thinning strands of his hair. As the admiral concluded his diatribe, the test director lifted his head and glared back. "Admiral, I'm just as frustrated as you are—maybe more. This baby is my company's pet project, after all." His eyes slid briefly to Col. Sinclair, and he cleared his throat. "I'm afraid we might have something here that is not computer originated."

"Spit it out, Archie," growled the admiral.

Archie took a deep breath. "I think someone is sabotaging the program, sir," he stated flatly. "I'd like permission to initiate— quietly—an investigation from the company's end. And, if possible, can you bring in the OSI to cover the military side?"

The admiral propped one hip against his desk and crossed his ankles. His eyes were still flinty. "You're talking sabotage?"

"Yes, sir. Have you ever heard of a virus program?"

Isaiah 59:9 (NIV): "So justice is far from us, and righteousness does not reach us. We look for light, but all is in darkness; for brightness, but we walk in deep shadows."

CHAPTER 1

Caleb Myers sat, sprawled as bonelessly as a cat, in the office of the president of Polaris Corporation. The company specialized in space tracking technologies and at present had a contract with the U.S. Air Force in Colorado. An agent for the Defense Security Agency, Caleb and Jackson Overstreet, the president of Polaris, had been friends for years. When Jack had asked for help, Caleb had made a few calls to the FBI agents in charge of the Starseeker case. With very little effort, he had been assigned to the case as a consultant, much to Overstreet's relief.

"I wish you'd given me a call eighteen months ago, Jack. From what you've told me today, the circumstances that resulted in the loss of your Navy contract sound as much like sabotage as the Starseeker case—even if you didn't think so at the time. Eighteen months ago I might have been able to track the source and saved your contract."

"Thanks," Overstreet muttered glumly. "My own security people aren't exactly slouches, you know, and all the clearances came through okay. We had no reason at the time to suspect any problems beyond faulty technology."

"Until your cancelled project turned up six months later in a rival company—no longer faulty."

"Until then. . ." the president repeated. He turned and picked up a bulging accordian folder from the top of his desk. Scowling at the contents for a moment, he finally held it out to Caleb, who rose lazily and took it.

"I understand there are three people who worked on that project who were assigned to Falcon?"

"Right." He suddenly jerked away from the desk, his palms slamming down on its waxed mahogany surface. "Cal, they've all been with Polaris five years or more! I pay them enough to keep them in a lifestyle an Arabian sheik would envy. It's *got* to be someone else!"

Caleb smiled in sympathy. Knowing your company was the unwitting tool in a nasty scheme to sabotage a top secret defense program was bad enough; having to face the probability of finding out the saboteurs were trusted employees twisted the knife that much deeper.

He slapped a commiserating hand on Jack's shoulder. "I'll fly down to the Springs tonight and get right on it," he promised. "Whatever the outcome, you don't want to lose another contract."

Jack summoned a wan smile. "You're right about that." He paused. "I'm sorry to spoil your vacation, Cal."

"Don't worry about it. My folks are used to it by now. I don't know why I wanted to visit Florida in March anyway. Water's still too cold for my old bones."

"Old bones, my great-aunt Matilda's favorite rocking chair." They grinned at one another with the familiarity of old friends.

Caleb tucked the accordian folder under his arm. "Take it easy, Jack," he counseled. "Don't worry yourself into an early grave. I'll report as soon as I can."

He drove back to his apartment with absentminded skill, so used to the maniacal Chicago traffic he could have been driving down a deserted country lane with the same sense of unruffled calm.

Three hours later he was in a plane, soaring through a night sky the color of his cat's sleek black coat. Relaxing back in the seat, Caleb found himself musing over the way God had directed the path of his life—and his current investigation. He didn't think his mother had ever quite reconciled herself to the fact that he had become ". . .an idealistic imitation of all those detective stories you used to read."

Mom had wanted him to be a minister. She couldn't accept that God had given him the talents and skills He had for any other purpose. But Caleb thought he understood. His mind was constantly on the prowl, wanting to understand, wanting to know more, wanting to know all the whys and wherefores, constantly analyzing. Several years of experience had taught him that his natural inquisitiveness was a distinct asset in this particular job.

With that reminder, he turned his thoughts to the problem ahead of him and his attention to the accordian file folder.

CHAPTER 2

It was late, a little before ten o'clock, when Rae Prescott finally pulled into the driveway of the red sandstone Victorian mansion she called home. Thin streams of moonlight fought their way through wispy clouds, casting shadows on the driveway and over the lawn. Located on a corner lot in the Old Colorado City district of the Springs, the turrets and gables that made the Prescott mansion a city landmark were visible only as dark, irregular shapes. Once again, Rae remembered that she had forgotten to replace the burned-out bulb in the back porch light. With a faint, exasperated mutter she turned off the engine and climbed out of her car.

Choir practice had run longer than usual, and her feet dragged up the few steps of the back porch. Easter was only three weeks away, but the church choir still sounded less than triumphantly joyful. As the keyboard accompanist for her church, Rae sympathized with the frustrations of Jerry, the long-suffering director.

Balancing on her hip the bag of groceries she had purchased on the way home, she fumbled in her purse for the back door key. All she wanted right now was a soothing mug of hot tea before she collapsed in bed.

A sudden rustle from the overgrown evergreen bushes to her right made her sigh in exasperation, and Rae plopped the sack and her purse down on the top step. For the last week a stray dog had been wandering around the neighborhood, eluding the Humane Society and ignoring annoyed residents who attempted to shoo him away. Calling softly, Rae urged, "Scram, mutt. I'm too tired to be nice to you tonight."

There was no response, not even a growl or the sound of retreating paws in the stillness of the crisp Colorado night. Rae stood, listening in the wavering moonlight that did not penetrate the cold black shadows.

Grumbling under her breath, Rae poked through her shoulder bag until her fingers closed over a small can of mace. Stomping noisily back down the steps, her predominant wish was that the dog would run away. She had bought the mace for self-protection and hated to use it on a starving, homeless dog.

On the other hand, the DeVries across the street had two small children, and old Elijah Mortenson two houses down claimed the animal had tried to bite him when he went after it with a stick.

Stooping, Rae groped around until her fingers closed over a rock to make one more try at flushing her quarry. If the animal came after her, she could use the mace, although she hoped she wouldn't have to. She hurled the stone into the bushes, but instead of a dog's bark, there came the sound of a muffled thud, followed by a rough, bitten off curse.

Rae froze as a dark, amorphous figure erupted from the bushes. A black-smeared face turned directly toward Rae. She held the can of mace in front of her extended arms and opened her mouth to scream.

The man tore off across the lawn and disappeared behind the house. A few seconds later Rae heard the faint scrunching sound of his footsteps fleeing across the street. The panicked scraping sound echoed loudly in her ears, pounding in rhythm with her stampeding pulse.

After a long moment of tense silence, she lowered her arms and retraced her steps. Picking up her purse and groceries, she let herself inside and shut the door, sliding home the bolt and fastening the safety chain.

Setting the groceries on the counter in her kitchen, she shrugged out of her coat and hung it on the bentwood coatrack in the corner. As if nothing out of the ordinary had happened, she methodically put all the groceries away.

Only then did she reach for the phone to call the police, but she pulled her hand back. What could she tell them? It had been too dark to see anything beyond the fact that it had been a large hulk of a male. She took a quick five minutes to check both the store and her living quarters. As near as she could tell, he hadn't broken into the house.

Chewing on her bottom lip, she returned to the galley-style kitchen, and, after another moment of indecision, called the police. While she waited for the patrol car, she cleaned the dishes out of the sink, then made a cup of hot tea, deliberately ignoring her trembling fingers.

The police officer, a tall, hard-looking man, walked around the entire house. There was no evidence of a break-in. He walked back up the porch steps where Rae waited in the doorway.

"We'll keep a patrol check in the area for awhile," he promised her. "But that's about all we can do right now—hiding in your bushes is not considered a crime since your yard isn't fenced in." One corner of his mouth lifted. "That foot-high stone wall doesn't count as a fence."

Rae shook her head. She was still off balance, amazed at the officer's casual acceptance of what, to her, had been an unnerving, frightening occurrence. Of course, her world and his had about as much in common as hard metal rock and a Mozart sonata.

"You mean he—or anybody else—can skulk around in my bushes, and I can't do anything?" Her voice rose, and she bit her lip. "What about trespassing?"

Light from the hallway streamed out the open door, glinting off the patrol officer's badge, and the butt of the revolver at his waist where one hand idly rested. He glanced up at the burned out porch light, frowning. "You ought to fix that," he said, mildly, ignoring her question. "Miss Prescott, we have one of the largest ratios of citizens to police officers of any depart-ment in the country. I'd like to be able to promise you a life of protected security, but anymore that's just not possible."

He glanced beyond her, down the angled hall with its golden oak walls and turn-of-the-century sconces. "I've always liked this old place," he commented. "I take it one of your ancestors built it since your last name is Prescott."

"My great-grandfather."

He nodded, then subjected her to a thorough, but detached scrutiny. "You do realize that a woman living alone has to be especially careful?"

Rae's chin lifted. Not for the world would she let him guess how shaken she was. "Yes, I know," she said evenly, meeting his gaze with a steady look. "I've lived here since I was a child."

"But not by yourself, right?" he turned, started down the steps, then paused to look back up. "Just remember what I told you. A prowler is a nebulous call—unless and until there's a crime committed, there's not a lot we can do. Be careful—and call if you need us."

Father, if he doesn't leave in a hurry I'm going to say something I shouldn't. . . . "Thank you." She summoned up a smile.

Rae carefully re-bolted and chained the door after he left. She walked slowly back to the kitchen, but stood in the doorway, staring sightlessly at the old-fashioned appliances and the wooden cabinets she had finally repainted last month. She had left her mug of hot tea on the burnished maple parson's table, and now walked over to pick it up, pouring the cold remains into the sink.

Turning on the faucet, she rinsed the mug out. Eventually it registered that she was just standing there turning the object around and around under the running water. With a defiant jerk she turned the water off and made her way to her bedroom. Sinking down on the floor by the bed, she buried her face in her hands and tried to pray.

After a while, she rose determinedly and got ready for bed. That night, for the first time since she was five years old, Rae left a light burning all night long.

15

CHAPTER 3

Heavy gray clouds rolling sluggishly over the tops of snow-sprinkled mountains greeted her the next morning.

The weather suited Rae's mood. It occured to her that she should re-read the psalm about looking up toward the hills for help although, as she pointed out rather truculently to her persistent conscience, it wasn't going to be long before the clouds completely obscured those hills. There would doubtless be a snowstorm by afternoon.

After tugging on corduroy slacks and a cowl-necked sweater, she forced down an English muffin and juice, then went to open the store. Everything was quiet, serene. The terror of the previous night had receded to the realm of an almost forgotten nightmare.

Joyful Noise, Rae's store, specialized in religious and classical sheet music. It comprised the front of the mansion, with her living quarters taking up the back rooms. She had closed the upstairs off after Uncle Floyd died to conserve heating costs. Between the store's income, the salary from the church, and the piano students three afternoons a week, she was just able to keep the wolf away from the door. Considering all the fears and doubts of those first couple of years, she felt almost smug right now. It had been a struggle, but she had done it.

As she crossed the huge parlor to flip the Open/Closed sign, she was startled to find a woman waiting outside the double oak doors. Apparently the threat of bad weather had persuaded customers to run their errands early. The woman was scowling, although the mantel clock was only now beginning to chime nine o'clock.

"Good morning," Rae offered, dragging open the heavy doors after she finally forced the stubborn, antiquated lock to release.

16

"Morning." The woman, a statuesque brunette in her early forties, darted a quick inquisitive glance around the room. Her sharpish brown eyes came back to rest on Rae. "I don't know much about music—I'm just trying to do a favor for a friend. I need a copy of—" she whipped out a folded piece of paper and glared at it, "—Schubert's *Marche Militaire*, it looks like."

"That will be in this room." Rae gestured to the large front room where she kept the classical music.

The woman looked at the music as if it were a scroll filled with Egyptian hieroglyphics, and Rae supressed a smile as she rang up the purchase.

A few minutes later a couple of music teachers Rae knew from Guild meetings bustled in to poke and prod in the bins. Then a young man stopped by looking for some contemporary Christian songs he could adapt to guitar.

Rae helped him find something he could work with, just as she helped the majority of customers who entered the store. She was possessive of the music, she knew, and tried hard not to hover. After three years she was doing better, but there was still that occasional lost sale because she hated letting people paw haphazardly through her treasures. It was a secret point of pride that she knew almost to the sheet where every piece of music was located.

She heaved a sigh of relief when the tinkling doorbell announced the departure of a mother with two preschoolers a little before lunch. A man held the outer door for them before entering the store himself. Rae, busily restoring the scattered music in the small popular section, glanced over her shoulder and smiled.

"Be with you in a minute," she called.

"No hurry," the man returned in a pleasant baritone. "I just wanted to look around."

Rats, Rae thought. *Another browser.* While she didn't begrudge the rights of consumers, Joyful Noise was not to the point where she felt financially free. Her brother Frank, a fairly successful

New York stockbroker, reminded her in his infrequent communications that she was an idealistic fool to struggle this way. Rae would quietly remind him that at least she had successfully saved their heritage, even if he was determined to deny they had one.

With an almost eerie echo of those thoughts, the man walked over to the small circular alcove, his gaze roaming appreciatively over the handcarved San Domingo mahogany and golden oak woodwork. "This place is fantastic. Do you know anything about its history?"

Rae straightened, wiping her hands on her hips as she got her first good look at him. Warm, ginger ale colored eyes framed by unfairly thick eyelashes smiled into hers. His hair, slightly wavy and unruly with a lock falling over his left eyebrow, was the color of nutmeg, a delicious blend of brown and blond and maybe a hint of auburn. In sunlight it would be stunning.

He was probably shy of six feet, but Rae felt oddly dominated by his presence in the confining space. She moved around him and back into the parlor area. "I'm very familiar with the history," she told him with a reciprocal smile. "I've lived here most of my life."

"Oh?" One thick eyebrow lifted and disappeared in the unruly lock of hair. "Was it difficult, turning it into a store?"

Something about this man warned Rae he was not as casual as he appeared. A distinct current seemed to radiate from him. She found herself watching his hands as he unbuttoned his trenchcoat. They were not the slender, pampered hands of a man who spent his day sitting behind a desk. Long, strong-looking, blunt fingertips were topped by neatly trimmed nails. *I bet he'd play a mean Grieg Concerto*, Rae mused distractedly.

Whoever he was, she didn't believe he had merely stopped by to browse.

"Are you a fan of late Victorian architecture?" she asked.

There was the slightest of pauses, the time it took for a moth to flutter its wings once, before the man nodded. "Amateur league only," he added. "That staircase is a masterpiece, isn't it?" He strolled over to run his hand over one of the elaborately carved griffins guarding either side of the stairs. After glancing up at the stained glass window on the landing, he turned back to Rae. "Mind if I go up?"

"I've closed it off," Rae said, hoping she sounded appropriately apologetic. "It costs too much to maintain it when I—" she stopped abruptly, unwilling to reveal the fact that she lived alone. Maybe it was last night's prowler, or perhaps it was only the undercurrent of poised alertness emanating from this man. She adopted what she hoped was an expression of professional blandness. "You're welcome to look around the store if you like."

The bell jangled, and with craven relief, Rae turned to the new customer, an older man who wanted to select a solo to sing at his church. Rae spent the next few moments helping him look. She was smiling and pleasant and professional, all the time feeling as if a peregrine falcon were hovering, waiting for just the right moment to swoop down on her.

Out of the corner of her eye, she marked the amber-eyed man's progress. He strolled, hands now thrust in the hip pockets of his worn, faded jeans, looking for all the world as if he were merely admiring the architecture.

But when the soloist was finally paying for his selection, the other man came and stood behind him at the counter. Casually removing his hands from his pockets, he began absentmindedly twisting the gold band of his watch. His gaze seemed lost in the middle distance.

Rae took her time ringing up the purchase, and went so far as to walk with the chatting soloist to the door. After returning behind the counter, she carefully noted the specifics of the sale in her log book. "Was there something you wanted?" she finally asked, without raising her head.

The man leaned over, resting his elbows on the high wooden counter. Rae suppressed the urge to scoot backward.

"No," he spoke very gently. "I just want to tell you how much I admire your family home, and—" his head tilted to one side as he gave her a somber, penetrating look that would haunt Rae for days, "—to remind you to be careful." He nodded toward the door with the sign stating 'Private—Keep Out.' "Do you live here alone?"

The pen dropped to the hardwood floor, clattering loudly on the scarred surface. Rae lifted her chin, pushed a strand of straight, honey-colored hair back up into the loose chignon she had pinned this morning. "Why do you want to know?" she asked with forced calm.

He straightened and shrugged. "Just wondered. This is a big house, located on a side street. You seem a little. . .on edge?"

Rae straightened and regarded him with stormy eyes. "I'm perfectly fine," she enunciated with crisp precision. "I just didn't. . .sleep too well." Her right hand, resting on the forgotten ledger, began unconsciously playing a Liszt rhapsody.

Suddenly he grinned, a wholesome, boyish grin that revealed a slightly chipped front tooth. The smile was so free of artifice and deceit that Rae responded in spite of herself. "I noticed your plaque over the fireplace," he said, "so I trust you know there's no reason for you to worry. Like it says, we're promised that His angels are guarding us in all our ways."

Before Rae could gather her scattered senses, he was gone, the cheerful tinkling of the bell lightly bouncing behind him.

Caleb opened the door of the rundown but clean motel room he was renting by the week. Shrugging out of his coat, he tossed it on the bed with one hand while the other reached for the phone.

After placing the call, he retrieved a small black notebook from the pocket of his trenchcoat, then made himself comfortable on the sagging bed, propping both pillows against the headboard.

Flipping through the notebook, he swiftly reviewed his notes, a resigned scowl faintly wrinkling his forehead. Then he picked up a ballpoint pen and jotted an additional note. "Checked out mansion—actually music store. Owner woman—early to mid-twenties. Nervous." The wary gray eyes had watched him even when she was waiting on another customer.

Caleb paused, tapping the end of his nose with the pen. He was irritated when his thoughts stayed on Rae Prescott instead of the Starseeker case. He had never had trouble concentrating before, but something about that lady played over his mind like a record needle stuck in a groove.

Lady. . .that's what it was. She reminded him of—not a Victorian lady—but an Edwardian one. Genteel, refined—but strong. He knew he had intimidated her, but she hadn't backed down. He liked that.

. . .He did not like liking that, though, and forced his thoughts back to his notebook and the case.

He'd been blessed with a photographic memory and didn't need to write anything down, but going through the motions usually helped pull together the missing pieces in most of his cases. He flipped back a few pages and re-read some notes he'd made several days before. His scowl deepened as he began to write again. "F. been twice. Innocent or planned? P.M. watch starting tonight."

He hoped, for the woman's sake, that the surveillance would turn out to be boringly routine. He found himself hoping as well that she had understood the oblique reassurance he had offered when he paraphrased the verse from Psalms.

CHAPTER 4

The snowstorm left a little over two inches. Just enough to turn the surroundings into a winter wonderland postcard, Rae thought with delight the next morning.

She stood on the back steps gazing out into the yard, where sculptured dollops of sparkling white icing coated the low brick wall, the tree branches...the bushes where the prowler had hidden the other night.

Her smile fading, Rae tightened her grip on the handle of the snow shovel and proceeded to clear off the steps and a path to the detached garage. She would have to hurry. She only had an hour before time to open the store.

Dry and light, the snow flew in a shower of sunlit powdered sugar as she shoveled. Across the street, Mr. DeVries emerged from his house, briefcase in hand, and they exchanged waves. Pausing for breath, Rae watched as his car backed out and drove cautiously down the plowed street. Her eye wandered over the pristine white blanket of her yard, as yet unmarred by footprints—

At first she couldn't quite believe it. Dropping the shovel, she took a hesitant step, then tugged off a mitten to rub a hand over her eyes. They were still there. Her breath escaping in sharp, stabbing puffs of icy steam, she walked with the slow gait of a somnambulist toward the bushes. Following the contours of the house, a set of faint but definite footprints left a silent, terrifying trail. They disappeared around the jutting covered porch that used to be the front entrance.

Disbelief warring with dread, Rae carefully traced them around to the brick pathway leading down to the sidewalk that bordered the street. The prints disappeared at the curb, obliterated by the snowplow.

She called the police with chill detachment, and sat on the front steps, arms wrapped around her knees and eyes frozen on the footprints until the squad car pulled up.

"...So I decided the store could wait a few minutes—I needed some old-fashioned tea and sympathy to bolster my courage. Even if the tea is cider." Rae wrapped her hands around the stoneware mug her best friend Karen had filled with hot apple cider and tried to smile.

Karen always looked like a model, even at eight o'clock in the morning. Right now, thanks to Rae, she looked more like a model for a murder mystery. Her huge blue eyes were wide with astonishment and her lithe, energetic body was tense with dismay and indignation.

"They told you the same thing they did last time? That there isn't a law against people poking and prying around your house like that, and just to continue to be careful?" Karen's slow southern drawl was markedly absent, her arms flapping in a brightly colored caftan like an agitated bird of paradise. "I think you better move in with me—at least for awhile—let me finish, now." She overrode Rae's denial. "I'm only two blocks down so it's not like you'd be abandoning the place to the creep who's creeping around."

Rae's answering laugh was hollow. "Karen, I willingly dropped out of school and gave up a career as a concert pianist to keep from selling the Prescott family home. Do you honestly think I'm going to slink away and hide in a corner just because some weirdo is trying to scare me?"

"*Trying,* honey?"

Rae's fingers were running furiously up and down Karen's glass-covered tabletop. "All right, so I'm scared. But I'm not going to run." Her expression matched her voice—composed and determined. With a frustrated sigh Karen capitulated.

"She who runs away lives to run another day," she misquoted darkly. She watched Rae for a minute, then sighed. "What are you playing this time?"

23

Rae's fingers clenched, and she slid them guiltily down under the table. "Bach," she confessed. *Bach when I'm only nervous. I wonder who I should try the next time I'm scared out of my skull?*

She swiped the last crumbly Danish from the plate and waved it with a flourish. "I can do all things though Christ," she claimed with some of Karen's dramatic flair. She took a bite of the Danish, grimaced, and decided two had been enough after all. "Oh, all right. . .stop looking at me like that. I'm quite aware of my shortcomings—you're constantly pointing them out. But seriously, Karen, I'm not trying to be stupid or heroic—I'm trying to be realistic. The police officer told me the guy could be anything from a prankster to a peeping tom to a careful cat-burglar since no attempt has been made yet to break into the house or the store. I pull all my shades at night—always have. So if he's a peeping tom he ought to give up soon. If he's out to rob me, and he's that determined, eventually he'll succeed—but I can't spend the rest of my life cowering somewhere while I wait for the worst to happen. I want to try to stay as—as normal as possible."

Her hands were back on top of the table, mindlessly playing a furious but soundless melody. "I'm praying a lot more fervently, perhaps—hoping God will be willing to dispense a few extra guardian angels to protect me from all those deep shadows and things that go bump in the night." Unbidden, there welled up in her the memory of a compelling stranger speaking similar words, in a voice as mellow and warm as golden honey.

She had not mentioned the incident to Karen, because after surviving a messy heartbreak two years earlier, Karen was rapidly turning into a rapacious manhunter. She would be after a man like that oboe-voiced stranger faster than snow melting on the radiator. She would also hound Rae to death.

With characteristic determination, Rae thrust the intrusive memory from her thoughts. She began braiding the tangled, almost waist-length strands of her hair, her fingers clumsy with frustration. She told herself—not for the first time—she was going to have this mess all cut off. She chewed at her bottom lip. "The police want me to take all of Uncle Floyd's and Aunt Jeannine's keepsakes, box them up, and put them in temporary storage," she confessed, taking the bobby pins Karen dug out of a nearby drawer for her and securing the braid around her head.

"I told you it was asking for trouble, leaving them on display in the store," Karen said. "You put all the ones your uncle gave you out there, too, didn't you?"

"What good are they if people can't enjoy looking at them? I've gotten lots of compliments, which makes the risk worthwhile. And it keeps the store from looking so—so commercial. Besides, I always hated the way Uncle Floyd hoarded them away upstairs."

"They'd do a thief or dope addict a lot of good. Bring 'em a pretty penny on the black market. It's still a marvel to me that one of your customers hasn't filched anything."

Rae shrugged. "I'm not going to worry about it. They're valuable, yes, but it's the house that I really care about. Sometimes I even wish—" she stopped. She would not blame Uncle Floyd, who had loved her and Frank as if they had been his own children. His character might have been flawed, but who was she to judge, especially considering her own past? "I'd better go. We both have to get to work. Tell Sylvia the Danish were scrumptious. Between the two of you, Gibson Girl is going to outshine every other restaurant in Old Colorado."

"What—not the entire city of Colorado Springs?" Karen gave her a brief hug but did not badger her any further about her decision. Rae was grateful, and after promising to call that evening, marched with firm tread back up the street.

She barely noticed the broad-shouldered man strolling along the sidewalk on the other side. He stopped, stuffing bare hands in the pockets of a blue and yellow ski jacket as he leaned casually against the eighteen-nineties lamp pole.

Rae glanced across the street, but kept on walking, too intent on her own thoughts to feel a pair of eyes burning a hole in her back.

Customers were sparse that day, even though the sun came out and melted most of the snow by late afternoon. It was a teaching day, and her students could enjoy her full attention. Most of it, anyway.

The large, sunny room behind the cash register had become Rae's studio; a local music store leased to her the grand she used for teaching. She had had folding doors installed that could be closed whenever there were customers.

Her students learned quickly not to waste time if Rae had a customer. Three-and-a-half rigorous years of training at Juilliard had endowed her with the fine-tuned ability to hear and correctly identify the note a chime was playing on a church bell six blocks away. The guilty student who fiddled around playing "Chopsticks" would usually end up practicing extra scales as penance.

It was a good thing her income was multi-faceted, Rae mused that evening, for she had made only four sales all day.

A retired couple traveling through the area bought a collection of Chopin waltzes and a teacher's choice grouping of short classical works for their granddaughter.

A balding, stoop-shouldered man who had come in a couple of times before returned to query her about early editions of Beethoven's works. Apparently he collected old sheet music, though he didn't play himself. Rae found him a couple of Schirmer editions and he departed, pleased.

Three giggling teenagers trooped in just before five o'clock and rearranged most of the popular music.

After Rae flipped the sign to "closed," she spent almost an hour putting the store in order. It was dark outside, the blood-red sunset evaporating into a frigid, frosty evening with typical Colorado abruptness.

Rae worked with only the floor lamp by the cash register on

for light. The store was almost ominously quiet with the departure of her last student, and the lamp cast grotesque, jagged shadows over the room.

Her head still ringing from the discordant notes of an energetic but unskilled student, Rae at first didn't notice anything unusual. She tucked the last piece of music back in its proper place, then moved behind the counter to tally the meager receipts of the day.

The scraping, shuffling noise was faint, but when the sound finally filtered through, Rae froze where she was standing. She felt as if a ham-sized fist had jammed her ribcage so she couldn't take a breath; her throat was so tight she couldn't swallow. With shaking fingers made clumsy from icy numbness, she very slowly zipped the cash inside the money pouch, then forced herself to turn off the light.

The room plunged into blackness simultaneously with the sudden barking of a dog from beneath one of the portico windows.

Dizzy with relief and a surging anger, Rae slammed the ancient cash register drawer shut and stomped through the door leading to the back of the house. She twisted the key furiously, rattling the door as she locked it. After depositing the money in the hidden safe Uncle Frank had installed almost forty years earlier, she swarmed into her bedroom.

She was so angry—both with herself and that wretched dog— that she could have chewed up a steel beam. She changed into jeans and a sweatshirt, tossing the ridiculously expensive six-year old angora dress on the bed. This aging evidence of her uncle's thoughtless extravagance just made her angrier.

Cleaning house for an hour helped a little.

Reciting her favorite Bible verse aloud ten times helped a little more. At least now she felt sheepish as well as angry and afraid. *Which hurts you the most, Lord? The anger or the fear?*

Supper and a hot bath still did not completely relax her. The food stuck in her throat and tasted like wads of crumpled paper.

The steam from the bath threatened to choke her, and her limbs felt as twitchy as the tail of a cat.

I will not let this situation defeat me, she vowed as she tightened the belt of her robe. *Lord, you've given me courage when I needed it before, and with your help I know I can handle this, too.*

Her steps faltered only a little as she padded wraith-like to her private music room. The ebony Steinway grand Uncle Floyd had given her at her high school graduation stood in solitary splendor in the middle of the room.

Sitting down, she opened the lid, adjusted the bench, and began to play. It was a long time before the music worked its magic on her jangled nerves.

CHAPTER 5

Saturdays in the store were usually Rae's busiest days, in spite of the winter season when the tourist trade was down and most of her customers were locals.

She hummed snatches of gospel songs and contemporary Christian music while she alternately waited on customers and watched a cold, drizzling rain splatter the windows. Even the dreary day did not dim her revived spirits. It had been a quiet, uneventful week. No stray dogs, no break-ins, no prowlers, and Rae's peaceful mood spilled over onto her smiling customers.

Late in the afternoon a woman entered the store, the silver bangle bracelets wreathing her wrists tingling along with the shop's bell. "I need a copy of Beethoven's Fifth," she said. "You know—the one with *Ode to Joy*." She hummed the first few phrases in a low contralto made raspy from too many cigarettes. "That's always been one of my favorites."

Rae opened her mouth to correct her, then stopped. "Don't I know you?" she asked as she led the woman to the classical music. "You look familiar." She selected an easy version with *Ode to Joy* printed in large letters across the top, and with an apologetic smile handed it to the woman. "I'm not good with faces, so I hope my bad memory won't keep you from returning to Joyful Noise."

The woman gave the music a cursory glance. "I've been here a time or two," she admitted.

She looked impatient, so Rae rung up the purchase and did not try to chat further. The woman thanked her and left, leaving behind the acrid cigarette odor that had been clinging to her clothes. Maybe the next time, Rae thought, she could tactfully point out that *Ode to Joy* was the choral symphony from Beethoven's Ninth, not his Fifth.

29

After closing the store for the day, she walked down the street to the Gibson Girl. Karen had converted a turn-of-the-century cottage into a cozy restaurant, decorated in the style of Charles Dana Gibson's "girl drawings." Copies of work from old issues of *Collier* and *LIFE* were framed and hung on the mauve painted walls. Waiters and waitresses dressed in period clothes, and there was even an old gramophone scratching out tinny turn-of-the-century tunes.

Rae let herself in the oval cut-glass door, depositing her dripping umbrella in a ceramic umbrella stand. Mouth watering odors and the pleasing sound of voices and clinking silver on china met her ears. Tugging off her gloves, she greeted Cheryl, the supper hostess, who led her to a corner table for two.

A cold draft of air blew around their ankles as the door opened behind them. The man who entered shrugged out of his blue and yellow ski jacket and hung it on the coat rack.

"I see you're as busy as Joyful Noise has been all day," Rae observed a few minutes later as Karen plopped down across from her. As they chatted, the drizzling rain accelerated to a downpour, and it was almost eleven when Rae finally told Karen goodnight. A rising wind from the southwest had finally pushed the clouds out onto the prairie, leaving behind a clear sky and rapidly dropping temperatures.

Shivering in her three-quarter wrap coat, Rae hurried up the street, head down against the wind. The streetlights glowed a hazy yellow, shining in the icy puddles dotting the street and sidewalks. Rae gave up trying to avoid them. Her leather boots would just have to be polished.

She crossed the dark, quiet street and started up the brick path. Towering Chinese elms blocked out much of the streetlight, and Rae suddenly wished she had borrowed Karen's flashlight after all. Annoyed at this lingering evidence of fear, she trod defiantly up the steps to the entrance of the store. She had left her Easter music underneath the counter and, regardless of the hour, planned to play through it—and the choir anthem—at least once.

Her hand froze just above the door handle. Someone was inside, moving around the religious music section with soundless stealth.

The very noiselessness raised the hair on the back of Rae's neck. Her disbelieving eyes followed the thin trickle of light playing over the music, watched it pause, flicker, then move across the hall toward the next room.

Clutching the lapels of her coat with stiff cramping, fingers, she chewed her lip, trying to decide what to do.

Sneaking back to Karen's to call the police seemed the safest, although the intruder could be gone by the time they arrived. She could try yelling to scare him off, but there was no telling what damage he might do to the store in his hurry to leave.

There was also no telling what damage he might do to her.

Fear and anger tugged at her with the same buffeting hands as the wind. Her ears ached; her nose stung, and her heart turned painful somersaults in her ribcage. She started to tip-toe back down the stairs, resigned to running back to Karen's, when her eyes, teared and blurred from the gusting wind, caught a furtive movement off to her left.

A dark form hurtled silently toward her. Its arms reached out like tentacles, poised for attack.

Rae's fingers were too clumsy inside her mittens. She was still fumbling in her purse when brutal hands closed over her forearms. Malodorous fumes of alcohol, tobacco, and sweat engulfed her as one of the hands shifted to cover her mouth.

Frightened and furious, Rae bit the hand and kicked at his legs. Twisting and struggling, she actually managed to free herself. She turned and ran, but her assailant caught her as she reached the street.

This time his hand fastened in her hair and yanked her head back. Bobby pins scattered and the braid unwound. His other arm wrapped around her waist and lifted her off her feet. Rae

31

felt as if her scalp was being torn off, and her body squeezed in two.

"Let *go* of me!" she gasped, and managed the beginning of a healthy scream before his hand clamped over her mouth again. She dug her elbow into a mushy stomach, and tried to claw his face with her fingers. The hand over her mouth dug into her jaw and smashed her lips, crushing her so brutally she was unable to bite. A harsh grunt grated into her ear when her flailing hand hit against a beard-roughened, fleshy cheekbone. The vise around her middle squeezed harder, driving out the remaining air in her lungs. Rae squirmed and struggled, but she was weakening rapidly.

Her blurring senses registered the sensation of movement to her right. Fearing it was the prowler in the store coming to the aid of his lookout, Rae renewed her struggles, the burst of adrenaline sending red spiralling sparks whirling behind the encroaching waves of blackness.

"What the—" The startled words disappeared in a grunt of pain. The hands holding Rae slackened.

She staggered, sucking air past a throat so constricted each inhalation stabbed like a thousand hot knives. Her limbs felt curiously weightless, yet weighed down with sandbags. In spite of all her willpower, her knees buckled, and she collapsed onto the wet sidewalk.

A battle raged two feet away. Her uncomprehending eyes watched her attacker and another darkly clad man exchange blows. The dull thud of fists hitting flesh was gratingly obscene; they fought in silence except for the harsh sound of their labored breathing.

Suddenly her attacker turned and fled, his huge body surprisingly fast. The fuzzy yellow of the streetlight wavered and dimmed: the man running away had the same hunched, shuffling flight as the prowler she had surprised in her bushes ten days earlier.

CHAPTER 6

The man who had come to Rae's rescue gave chase, but stopped at the corner of her house and turned back. Rae lurched to her feet. Her purse was gone, so she couldn't use the mace. *So much for my Wonder Woman routine*, she thought with lunatic calm. At least this time she could let loose with one good scream before—

"It's all right. I'm not going to hurt you. Please don't scream." The words were soothing, reassuring, but more goosebumps raced over Rae's bruised, stinging skin. She knew that voice as surely as she had known that the fleeing man had been the prowler.

"You?" She gaped, mouth slack. He approached her slowly, holding out his hand. Rae slapped it away. "Who are you?" Her throat was so raw it hurt to talk.

"Caleb Myers. If I'd had any idea this was going to happen, I would have introduced myself the other day in your store." He lifted his hand again, then dropped it when Rae stepped back and almost fell off the curb. "Miss Prescott, I'm not going to hurt you—let me help you inside so you can get warm."

She hadn't realized until he commented on it that she was shivering almost uncontrollably from the knifing wind as well as her assault. Tugging her coat closer, she glared at Caleb Myers. "Don't touch me. If you really wanted to help, you could have come to my rescue before that—that disgusting creep practically squeezed me in two."

She lifted a shaking hand to try to hold her hair out of her face. The braid had come unbound completely, and the wind was blowing hair all over her face, neck, and shoulders.

A corner of Caleb Myers's mouth twitched. "I was on the second story of the vacant house across the street. I got here as

33

soon as I could."

Rae bit her lip. "I'm sorry—and I do thank you. What—" A sudden gust of wind almost knocked her off her feet, and this time when Mr. Myers's hand shot out to steady her, she didn't jerk free. "Maybe we better go inside. My purse should be near the porch." She stopped. "What about the other man? There was one inside the store."

He squeezed her arm, a gentle reassuring squeeze. "I'll go check. Wait here."

"I most certainly will not," Rae snapped. "How do I know there's not a third man hiding somewhere? For that matter, how do I know *you're* not in cahoots with them?"

"I'm an agent with DSA—Defense Security Agency," the man replied patiently. "I've had your place under surveillance for almost two weeks now. If you'll allow me to check the premises, we can go inside and I'll explain."

Rae's chin lifted. "I want to see some identification."

There was a short pause. She was shaking so hard now she could not prevent her legs from quivering; all the feeling had left her hands and feet some time ago. But she was not going another step until this gentle-voiced, eagle-eyed man provided her with more proof than his brief explanation. *Why on earth does he have my home under surveillance? What's going on?*

She stared up into his shadowed face, a little disconcerted because in the shrouded moonlight it looked as though he were smiling.

He reached into the back pocket of his jeans and tugged out something that looked like a worn leather wallet. It wasn't. "Here." A small penlight appeared as if by magic and shone on an official looking ID with a badge on one side and a grainy head photo on the other. It stated that he was indeed Caleb Andrew Myers, and a resident of Chicago, Illinois. He had brn. hair, lt. brn. eyes, was 5'11", and weighed 177 lbs.

"Your eyes aren't brown," Rae said. "And there's red in your hair—especially when light is shining on it."

"The man typing out the information didn't have much imagination," Caleb Myers returned. He added very gently, "Miss Prescott, I think you need to go inside. But wait here, please, so I can check the place out. I'll be back in just a minute."

Rae shuddered as another gust of wind tugged at her coat and bit her ears. Maybe singing a song would take her mind off her circumstances. The one that came to her lips was an oldie about eyes.

She could lose herself in Caleb Myer's eyes, Rae decided. And the way he looked as if he were smiling even if he wasn't. . .what a rescue! *Thanks, Lord, for such an attractive guardian angel.*

She shivered again, and her voice cracked. Maybe singing wasn't such a good idea.

When Caleb Myers returned, his hand cupped Rae's elbow and ushered her up the steps. He had found her purse, and waited while she fumbled for the key. The patient expression did not alter when she removed the can of mace as well, and pointed it toward his face.

"It's a shame you weren't able to use that on your attacker," he commented easily. "Would you like me to unlock the door so you can keep me covered?"

Rae did not back down. "Yes. It's old and tricky, especially when it's cold." A little voice pointed out that she was behaving in a very irrational manner. Rae ignored the voice.

She watched him work the frustrating lock with irritating ease. "The first thing I'm going to do is call the police. Then I'll check my store."

"Whatever you say."

His voice was much too agreeable, Rae thought as they entered the dark store. Even with the heat turned down, the room was blissfully warm after the frigid night and blowing wind. She walked across the floor on still shaky legs and turned on the floorlamp. Caleb Myers followed, shrugging out of a thick, fleece-lined jeans jacket. In the brighter light, Rae studied him closely, and after a minute lowered her arm, placing the can of mace on the counter.

He was looking at her with such—such compassion that a painful blush heated her frozen, chapped cheeks. The wind had blown his hair into thick, unruly waves. It made him look tough, rakish, and aggressively male.

But with those piercing golden eyes studying her with that gentle compassion, Rae could not be afraid of him. Her gaze fell to his hands. One set of knuckles was scraped and had bled slightly.

"Your hand," she faltered, and he glanced down at it.

"I'm sure his jaw feels worse." He paused. "Your face is pretty bruised. Does it hurt yet?"

Rae lifted her fingers to explore her cheek and jaw. She winced. "Yes." She wriggled her shoulders, took a deep breath. "I'll call the police, then put on a kettle. Would you like some tea while you explain what you're doing spying on me, Mr. Myers?"

"Call me Caleb," he replied, ignoring the pointed remark. "If you'll show me your kitchen, I'll heat the water so you can look around your store after you call. Don't touch anything, okay? They'll want to dust for fingerprints."

After filling a tarnished brass kettle with water and putting it on an old gas stovetop to boil, Caleb prowled around Rae Prescott's living quarters while she checked out the store. The FBI guys had already confirmed that she had lived alone for the past three years since her paternal uncle died. There was an older brother, but no address was available yet.

In a room that looked like a cozy Victorian parlor, he found the only photographs in sight. One was of an elderly bearded man, cane in one hand, with the other arm wrapped around a younger Rae's shoulders.

Next to that photograph was a framed snapshot of a lanky

man with gangly arms and legs. He was standing next to a flashy red sports car, an expression of smug pride on his face. The same brown hair, long narrow nose and stubborn chin as Rae identified him as the brother.

Caleb looked on the back of the photo, but there was nothing written to corroborate his conclusion. He put it back down, smiling a little. Rae's arms and legs looked just about as long, slender, and unwieldy as her brother's. They had probably been teased unmercifully; Rae still moved with a sort of awkward grace, as though she had never quite learned what to do with all her limbs.

He continued his prowling, tucking away nuggets of information. No pets. Lots of plants. A mixture of antique and modern furniture, most of which needed dusting. Several framed Scripture verses like the one over the fireplace in the store. Most of these were from Psalms. The quiet proclamation of her faith to anyone who visited touched the vibrant chord in his own heart. Nodding to himself, he moved out of the parlor into another room.

It was her bedroom. A cursory search assured him that it was empty of intruders, though he did lift a brow at her crammed, overflowing closet. The quality of the clothes was top-notch, the majority of the labels those of world famous designers, though the styles were several years old at least. Not a single article was new. Caleb grinned at what his three sisters would have said about that sorry state of affairs.

Rae Prescott might have enjoyed material wealth in the past, but apparently those days were long gone. He found himself liking her even more because she accepted her present circumstances with such grace. Before he left the bedroom, he made a quick call from the phone on her bedside table.

The last room had no furniture except for a tremendous black grand piano. Music was piled everywhere. On the floor, in boxes, on the piano, on the bench by the piano.

Caleb smiled with self-directed irony, shaking his head as he quietly made his way back to the kitchen. He had conducted hundreds of investigations over the years. Most of them involved women at some point, and lots of them had been attractive, even beautiful. None of them ever registered beyond a professional level. He could call up a detailed physical description of any of them, but the memories didn't elevate his blood pressure.

Until now. Rae Prescott was not beautiful and made no pretensions otherwise, yet she made his blood pressure shoot skyward every time he looked at her. It was disconcerting, and puzzling—and impossible to ignore.

Rae was opening a tin and taking out two teabags. Her face, as he entered the room, was pale, hostile, the huge gray eyes smudged with suspicion.

"Did you enjoy your tour?" she asked, ripping open foil-covered tea bags and dumping them into a couple of mugs.

"I'm sorry." Caleb took the kettle and poured the water for them. "I needed to make sure you didn't have anybody hiding behind a door or in a closet."

He put the kettle back on the stove, and they sat down at an attractive maple trestle table. "I think I told you that your home is an impressive place, didn't I? I really like the way you've kept the integrity of the rooms in spite of turning half of them into a store."

"Thank you."

She sat there, glaring at him with wavering eyes as if she couldn't decide whether to smile graciously—or fetch that can of mace.

Caleb sighed. Rae Prescott might be a gutsy lady, but right now she looked ready to shatter. "I saw your Bible verses—they're some of my favorites."

He waited while she slowly registered the implication. "You know, we originally planned to discontinue the surveillance last night. But I had this feeling—now I know it was God's way of getting my attention—so I decided to watch one more night.

Now we know why, don't we?"

She stared across at him, the wide unblinking eyes filling with incredulous relief. "You're a Christian, too?" she whispered.

"Yes, I am. Will you try to trust me a little now, Rae Prescott? It will make the next weeks—and possibly months—a lot easier on both of us."

CHAPTER 7

The police were a lot more thorough than they had been the last two times. There were also a lot more of them. It was a multiple response, Caleb told her, in the hopes that the burglars could still be chased down and caught.

Some of the officers stayed outside to search the area, but it seemed as if her kitchen and store were suddenly overrun by a swarm of stone-faced, intent professionals. There were even a couple of men in rumpled civilian suits; they slipped in while Rae gave her account of the assault to a police officer holding a clipboard stuffed with report forms.

Caleb, after giving his statement and showing his ID, stayed out of the way. He and the two plainclothesmen clustered together in a corner of the store, talking quietly. Caleb looked relaxed, casual, as if he were discussing the latest Bears game with a couple of friends. Every now and then he looked across at Rae, and she would avert her head.

She sat on the stairs leading to the second floor. Legs pressed together, arms rigidly at her sides, she watched the beehive activity with the detached interest of a fourth grade boy observing an ant farm. The only time she spoke was to make a rather tart request that they please be careful not to disarrange the music.

After the swarm of police officers finished poking and prying around the store, the sandy-haired one who had written up Rae's account strolled over. With him was yet another arrival, a short, trim man with iron-gray hair and shrewd blue eyes. The police officer introduced him as Detective Pete Grabowski. He glanced toward Caleb while Det. Grabowski looked Rae over like a piece of fresh fruit at the farmer's market.

"Miss Prescott," he said, in a surprisingly deep tone, "I know you've given Officer Hanley your statement, but would you mind telling me what happened again? Try to remember every detail, regardless of how insignificant you think it is."

Rae stood up, still very calm. "I spent the evening with my friend Karen. She owns the Gibson Girl." The detective nodded, so Rae continued without elaborating, though she shuddered inwardly at what Karen's response would be to the events of this night. "I was walking home a little after eleven—I waited 'til the rain quit. When I was on the front porch, I saw someone inside."

"You've confirmed that to the best of your knowledge nothing has been stolen?"

She nodded, mouth quirking wryly. "It makes this whole mess more bewildering. What could they have wanted?"

One of the plainclothesmen who had been conferring with Caleb Myers walked over. Det. Grabowski turned and they spoke in low syllables Rae could not hear. The lines furrowing the detective's head deepened; when he turned back to Rae, she sensed a coldness, almost hostility.

"Miss Prescott," he spoke slowly, as if measuring each word, "you live here alone. . .you have on display in your store objects worth thousands of dollars, yet you have taken only the most rudimentary precautions to safeguard them. After the past few weeks, I find that extremely foolish."

"I don't have the funds necessary to install the alarms and newer locks your associates recommended." Robbing a bank would help, but she decided it might not be such a good idea to suggest that. She clasped her hands together to keep from playing Bach on the stair railing. "If someone wants to steal anything, they'll find a way regardless of any protective measures."

"And would you realize a substantial insurance settlement?" Det. Grabowski suggested softly.

Rae clutched the bannister to keep from swaying. "Are you implying—" she could not finish, but the detective followed through with the *coup de grace.*

"When was the last time you saw your father, Miss Prescott?"

It was such a totally unexpected question that Rae felt all the indignant color drain out of her face. Staring mutely at the gimlet-eyed detective, her fingers wrapped around the top of the griffin's head so tightly her knuckles gleamed bone-white.

"I've just been told your father is wanted by the FBI for a number of crimes," Grabowski pursued, still in that cold, level voice that raised welts on Rae's shrieking nerves. "Heading the list is grand larceny. Miss Prescott—is it possible that your lack of precaution is intended? That the open display of all these items is so your—"

"How are things going over here, Grabowski?" Caleb Myers moved between them, his eyes on Rae. "Miss Prescott doesn't look like she's holding up too well. Maybe the rest of it could wait until morning?"

"I'm fine—" Rae began, but she did not pull away from the hand urging her to sit back down on the stairs. It felt so warm, and she was so cold her teeth were chattering. She fastened her eyes on the melting sunshine of Caleb's gaze. At lease *he* didn't suspect her.

When he spoke again, his voice was as mild as a summer day, but Det. Grabowski suddenly looked a lot less intimidating. "That would give your people time to gather some mug shots for a photo line-up."

"Miss Prescott claims she wouldn't be able to recognize her attacker." Grabowski looked as if he wanted to debate that claim, but his eyes at least had lost some of the cold suspicion. "There won't be a line-up unless it's for you." He paused, then added with a deliberate lack of inflection, "Ramirez was just telling me about the background check on the Prescott family."

Caleb nodded. Suddenly he dropped down in front of Rae, balancing gracefully on the balls of his feet. All the sympathy was gone, and his look now was one of probing professionalism.

Rae didn't need or want this. . .this golden-eyed guardian angel fighting all her battles or speculating about her past. It was

42

none of his business. It was nobody's business, even if—

"Rae, tell me about your father," Caleb asked gently. His voice compelled rather than demanded; Rae felt her defenses collapsing.

"I don't know anything about my father," she admitted stiffly. "He deserted us when I was four."

"You haven't seen or heard from him since?"

"No." Her gaze slid up to Det. Grabowski. "I don't lie. And I don't defraud. What's more, I wouldn't realize a penny if anything were stolen because the only insurance I carry is for the house itself. Carrying a personal articles floater is not a financial option right now."

Det. Grabowski started to say something, caught Caleb's eye, and shut his mouth with a scowling snap. He looked impatient and more than a little disgusted.

"Rae," Caleb continued matter-of-factly, "the reason you might feel like you're on the wrong end of an interrogation is because you might be involved—unknowingly, of course—in a case I'm working on with the FBI, the OSI—and now the Colorado Springs Police Department."

"You're divulging information that might be inappropriate at this time, under the circumstances," Grabowski drawled.

Caleb rose, holding out his hand. After a minute Rae slowly put hers in it. "You just informed Miss Prescott that her father—a man she claims not to have seen since she was four— is wanted by the FBI. She deserves more than your suspicions, Grabowski."

"I fail to see what any of this has to do with my store being broken into and my being attacked." Rae's lips were stiff, and she had the unnerving sensation of being on trial. At least she had taken the time to twist her hair up in a chignon before the police arrived.

Grabowski and Caleb Myers exchanged glances; with an irritated swipe of his hand, Grabowski wordlessly yielded the floor to Caleb. Rae wondered if he got his way in everything he did. Before he could explain, one of Grabowski's men interrupted.

"We're all through here, sir." The young man who had been dusting for prints glanced sympathetically at Rae. She knew she looked awful, but her embarrassment took a back seat to her need to know. She waited while Det. Grabowski barked out orders and instructions. At last he turned to her.

"Mr. Myers obviously feels the need to enlighten you, Miss Prescott, so I will leave him to it." He paused, then added levelly, "You aren't planning to go anywhere in the next few weeks, are you?"

"No." She smiled sweetly. "I don't have enough money for a vacation, either."

CHAPTER 8

After everyone trooped out, leaving behind a ringing silence, Caleb tilted his head and grinned at her. "That wasn't too good an example of turning the other cheek, Miss Prescott."

Ashamed but defiant, Rae toyed with the buttons on her henley top. "I know. I thought I'd learned how to control my tongue, but I guess everything sort of overwhelmed me." She glanced at him, then away. "Mr. Myers—"

"Caleb."

Rae half-smiled. "Caleb. . .what's going on? I feel like I fell off the tour bus into the middle of a bad TV cop show." To her utter mortification, her voice broke on the last word. *Oh, no, not now, please. I've been doing so well.*

"Why don't we go back in the kitchen?" Caleb suggested. "It's a lot warmer. I'll re-heat the water, and we can have another cup of tea." His voice deepened with amusement. "I saw all your cannisters and cartons. You must stock every kind of tea on the market."

"Tea is a very versatile drink." She began to walk quickly ahead of him, surreptitiously dabbing her eyes. Whatever Caleb told her, she must maintain control. Control, her professor at Juilliard used to say, was everything.

Dear Father, please don't let me lose control. . . .

Caleb sprawled along the trestle bench, eyes hooded. He wondered how much to tell her, and if what he did tell her would finally shatter the formidable control. Idly fiddling with his watchband, he offered up a swift prayer as Rae deposited his mug of tea and sat down opposite him.

"I'm working with the FBI at the moment. A friend of mine owns a corporation specializing in the development of state-of-the-art space tracking technologies. He called and asked for my

45

help, and the FBI agreed to bring me in as a consultant." He grinned sheepishly. "I seem to have acquired something of a reputation in the field of computer fraud and sabotage."

He quit fiddling with his watchband and tugged on an irritating lock of hair instead. "Someone is sabotaging the contract Polaris has with the Air Force, and we have reason to believe the individual or individuals are long-time employees. I'm trying to help find out who it is. The OSI—that's the Air Force equivalent of the FBI—is handling the active duty guys, but the FBI gets the rest. Everyone's getting a little antsy since every official from the Defense Department down, both military and civilian, is screaming for results."

Rae sipped her tea. She would not look at him. "And you think my—my father is involved?"

"I don't know. Tonight is the first time I was informed of what they've found out so far on the background check." He took a sip of his own drink, and had to struggle to keep a straight face. She had given him some aromatic herb tea that tasted about like crushed dandelions. Swallowing the intense desire for an old-fashioned mug of hot chocolate, he manfully took another sip. He forgot about the bitter brew when Rae's face, already pale and strained, blanched even further. The ugly bruises stood out like smears of charcoal on a white sheet.

"The FBI has been checking up on me—on my family?" she repeated, her voice puzzled, wary.

Caleb suppressed the urge to cover her nervous fingers with his own. "I told you we've had your place under surveillance," he explained. "One of the suspects has come to your store several times the last few weeks. And on a routine check with the CSPD, we found out about the footprints in the snow. I guess Tray ordered the check. He's the FBI agent who's been assigned to head up the case locally. . . . What are you doing with your hands?"

The restless movements of her fingers stopped abruptly and her hands wrapped back around the mug. "Nothing," she muttered in a stifled voice. "And that's why you have my house under surveillance?"

Caleb did not pursue the matter of her hands. "We have to follow up on any lead, no matter how slim or ludicrous. So far, you represent the best contact yet. The suspect could be coming here just out of a love for music, but it could also be something else—especially after hearing about your prowlers."

Looking across at Rae, he noted dispassionately that she had finally started to calm down, though her face beneath the darkening bruises was still pale. "I told Tray I'd cover the night shift." His mouth dented in a wry grin. "Stakeouts are the worst duty to draw. Guys go to any lengths to avoid them because they're boring, tedious, and it's impossible to maintain a constant vigilance and keep your sanity."

"So why did you volunteer?"

Caleb shrugged. "My mind is too active to get bored very often. And when I get sleepy—I pray out loud. It always helps. The FBI takes over during the day. I sleep four or five hours, then follow my own leads."

He pushed aside the tea as a lost cause, then steeled himself to admit candidly, "I blew it tonight—had no idea there was anyone over here."

"According to the police, they came in a window on the side. You wouldn't have been able to see even if it wasn't dark." Her voice broke again, and she lifted her head at last. "Caleb, would you excuse me a few minutes? I—I need to be alone."

He stood, watching with a frown between his eyes as she stumbled gracelessly out of the kitchen. If it had been any other woman, he would have offered the comfort of his shoulder. He had had to console three younger sisters all his life, in all sorts of circumstances ranging from skinned knees to heartbreak.

Mom kept telling him his soft heart would get him something beyond a soggy shoulder one day. . . .

Caleb knew that day might have arrived. Sitting back down, he mentally added up everything he had learned about her since

47

their first, inauspicious meeting almost two weeks ago. He was not encouraged. *Lord, what do I do with a very independent, very vulnerable woman who looks like she might have been tossed in the middle of a hornet's nest?*

And what would he do if Ray Meikleham Prescott *had* decided to return to his daughter's life? Caleb mulled over everything Tray Ramirez had told him, and decided that, regardless of the thorns, he would have to try his best to protect the prickly Rae Prescott. Right now she definitely could not be compared to a sleek Siamese. She was more like the delicate, spindly cat's claw wildflower that grew in such abundance in the meadows behind his parent's Florida panhandle home. Dainty and flimsy to look at, the stems were covered with minute hooked thorns that could lacerate anyone unwary enough to try to pick them

A grin kicked up the corner of his mouth. He had a strong hunch he better not share any of his fanciful descriptions of her with Rae.

Rae Prescott. And Ray Meikleham Prescott, her father. The grin faded as he realized the Starseeker case had just corkscrewed again. His ever-restless brain began its automatic examination and sifting process. Thanking God once again for His gifts, Caleb allowed his memory to search and bring up everything he had read about individuals involved with IOS. If Rae's father was involved, Caleb planned to find out how and why.

CHAPTER 9

She couldn't sleep. After tossing and turning and watching the clock until the illuminated hands passed the hour of two, Rae threw back the covers. Picking up the poker she had placed by the bed, she turned on every light as she made her way to her music room.

For awhile she played old gospel songs, hymn arrangements, even the music from the Easter musical. Her fingers flowed over the keyboard, and the music filling the lonely night might have made the angels rejoice, but it didn't help Rae. After thirty minutes she sighed and rose. It would have to be classical. Nothing else was complicated enough, challenging enough to keep her mind from churning over the events of the evening.

Maybe it was the unconscious memory of the woman surfacing, but Rae decided to play Beethoven's Ninth Symphony. The soaring "Ode to Joy" would remind her of God's eternal watchcare. She might as well play the Fifth, too, while she was at it.

A brief search through the cluttered piles of music did not yield either one, and Rae didn't feel like pawing through piles the rest of the night. She let herself into the store, swallowing a painful lump of uneasiness. With all the police around here earlier, even a half-wit criminal would know better than to break in a second time. She hoped.

Everything looked normal, in order. It wasn't. All her copies of Beethoven's Fifth and Ninth Symphonies were gone.

"Whaddaya think, Myers? Both father *and* daughter—it's too much to be coincidence."

Tray Ramirez paced back and forth across a threadbare, dirty gray carpet, his normally pleasant face creased in a scowl. Thick black hair and an olive skintone attested to his Latin heritage.

49

"Maybe she's innocent and really hasn't seen her old man in twenty years or so, but you gotta admit Miss Prescott is in this thing up to her dainty little ears."

"I'm convinced the involvement is planned—but not by Rae. She was blown away when Grabowski dropped the bomb about her father." Caleb kept his voice lazy, almost indifferent. The more uptight other people became, the more low-key he projected his own emotions.

"She could be a good actress."

Caleb shook his head decisively. He remembered with unusual clarity a pair of gray eyes almost unfocused with pain and shock, a wide mouth that trembled in spite of concerted efforts to keep it still. "I don't think so. She was attacked, assaulted, and on her way down when I rescued her." He grinned. "That didn't faze her—she ripped a strip off me for taking so long to get there—even went so far as to point a can of mace in my face. When I came back after searching the store, she was singing."

Ramirez stopped at his desk, white teeth flashing in a reciprocal smile. "I admit she's a little unorthodox. . . .Did you see her stand over one of the police officers and lecture him for not being careful with her music? But I fail to see—"

"When Grabowski told her about her father, I thought she was going to pass out." Caleb shoved the irritating hair off his forehead, then leaned forward in the chair where he had been sitting. "Tray, she's an innocent victim. We've got to protect her, not persecute her."

The FBI agent slammed his hand down on the desk. "You tell me how, man! We've had men watching the store—*you've* been taking the nights for two weeks—and none of us spotted anything!" He paused, adding heavily, "You do realize that your timely rescue will raise more questions with the wrong people? If the Prescott woman is a dupe, your interference is going to make her situation even worse."

Caleb's fingers slid under the watchband and restlessly

twisted. "I know. IOS doesn't care who gets in the way."

"You're convinced they're behind this? According to my reports, they don't like going after the U.S. government." His mouth twitched. "We have more money and manpower than most of the local cops."

"I know, but the *m.o.* is too similar to another program Polaris was perfecting with the Navy a couple of years ago." Caleb laced his hands behind his head. "A program cancelled due to supposedly faulty software that turned up later in a company with definite IOS connections."

"I don't like it," Ramirez said reluctantly. "Until we get a confirmed lead on one of the Starseeker personnel, we're walking in traffic blindfolded and handcuffed."

"I'm going to talk to Rae Prescott again. She might have remembered something now that she's had a night to sleep on it."

"You say you didn't recognize the assailant either?"

Caleb shook his head, and rose. "He wasn't one of the three we've been keeping tabs on, no." He headed for the door, adding very softly, "But you can be sure I'll recognize the gentleman again."

"What do you want?" Rae finished pulling the doors shut, muffling the sound of Angela MacVeese playing a spirited boogie.

Caleb Myers cocked his head toward the room behind her. "You teach piano lessons as well as run Joyful Noise?"

"You mean you didn't know? I'm also the accompanist for our church—and if you like I can show you my driver's license, although you probably know all that information, too."

He smiled slowly, a dazzling smile warm enough to melt concrete. "Well, I must say I hadn't exactly hoped for the fatted calf, but I didn't expect a verbal assault, either."

His eyes moved over her, and Rae had a feeling he was memorizing every bruise and freckle. Right now they were mostly suffused by the blush creeping over her face at Caleb's gentle chastising. "I didn't sleep very well, and I *am* in the middle of a lesson. I'm sorry if I sounded. . .brusque."

He walked over to stand directly in front of her. Rae looked up at him, refusing to step back even when his hand lifted. His fingers skimmed with the lightness of gauze over her bruised face. "Hurt pretty bad?"

"Only when I smile, which is another reason I'm being such a grouch." They both grinned then, though Rae could not suppress the accompanying wince. "Everyone thinks I'm extremely lucky."

"You were. Though I'd call it something besides luck."

She focused on the strong-looking tendons of his throat. "I know," she whispered. With a brisk shake of her head, she turned around and slid the door open a crack. "Angela, remember to practice feeling the rhythm. Emphasize the left hand a little more. I'll be there in a minute." She turned back to Caleb, in control once more. "I do have to go."

"I need to talk to you. Can I stop by when Joyful Noise closes and take you out to dinner?"

"I don't—"

"It concerns your father, Rae."

Though the words were spoken gently, she sensed the force of will behind them. He was circling her patiently, but if she didn't fall in with his wishes, Rae had no doubt that he would take her arm and usher her out the door. Feeling resentfully like a rabbit baring her throat to the striking talons of a falcon, she gave her consent. "Six-thirty, then. And just for dinner."

Laughing lights danced through his eyes. "Yes, ma'am, Miss Prescott."

Two hours later, she was flipping the sign to "Closed" when a man clad in a navy blue suit strode swiftly up the steps and came through the doors. "Miss Prescott?" He held up a badge. "Det. Jamison. Will you come with me to the station, please?"

Rae straightened and moved over to the the revolving popular music display to give herself time to think. "Someone is meeting me at six-thirty," she said as her hands began straightening music. "What did you need me at the station for? I was told this morning that I wouldn't need to come back."

"We brought in a suspect. We'd like to see if you recognize him."

Her hands stilled. She turned to the detective, hoping the apprehension was not showing too nakedly on her face. "I told Det. Grabowski I didn't think I'd be able to recognize him—it was too dark, and it all happened too fast."

Swift impatience crossed the detective's face. "Nonetheless, I want you to check out the line-up. If you'll come with me, you'll be back in plenty of time for your date." He held the door.

Rae did not correct his assumption. She could see an unmarked car parked at the curb with another suit-clad driver waiting behind the wheel. "Let me get my coat and purse."

She was uneasy, but followed the cold-voiced detective to the car. As she climbed into the back seat, Det. Jamison followed her and slammed the door. As the car pulled away from the curb, he turned to Rae. In his hand was a short, ugly-looking gun, and it was pointed straight at her heart. The car careened around the corner and sped down the street. As the driver twisted his head around very briefly, Rae's terrified stare jerked from the gun to the man's face. Her eyes widened in stunned recognition.

"I don't think," the bogus Det. Jamison stated softly, "that we need to make that trip to the station, do we, Miss Prescott?"

CHAPTER 10

"What do you want?" Rae asked. Her voice was eerily calm, almost polite. After the one heart-jerking glance at the driver, she kept her eyes fastened on "Detective Jamison," while her mind fought the question of how many interminable seconds she would suffer from a bullet at close range.

Her captor relaxed back in the seat, but the gun did not waver. "I'm a messenger, Miss Prescott." Suddenly he leaned forward and the cold barrel of the gun slid lightly over Rae's bruised cheeks. "A good-will messenger sent to keep you from acquiring any more of these."

Rae shrank back. "Greater is he that is in me. . ." she mumbled, her tongue unwieldy and her lips rubbery.

The man narrowed his eyes. "Shut up and listen," he stated with such flat coldness that Rae obeyed. Twining her icy hands in a death grip in her lap, she pressed her lips together and waited.

"If you want to stay healthy, Miss Prescott. . .and you want that ugly palace of yours to keep its present form. . .you'll keep your mouth shut about anything you see or hear today or in the future. You see nothing; you know nothing." He leaned forward again, crowding Rae against the car door so that her spine pressed painfully into the handle. "Including the identity of my acquaintance up front there. I know you recognized him." The cruel, thin lips bared in a macabre smile. "So just keep practicing that wide-eyed innocence. . .or next time he won't be as gentle with you."

Rae tried to lick her parched lips, but her mouth was too dry. "Who are you?" she demanded with husky bravado, then flinched when the gun waved a hair's breadth from her face.

"No questions, lady." His head swiveled sharply. "Slow down, you fool!' he rapped out furiously. "Do you want every

54

traffic cop in the Springs on our tail?"

The respite from the opaque deadness of his eyes was such a relief, Rae drew a shuddering breath, then started to lift a hand to her hair. Like a striking rattlesnake, the man's head whipped around and his free hand shot out. It closed around her wrist and twisted, causing Rae to gasp in pain.

"Unless you want to be dumped on your back doorstep in a trash bag, keep your hands in your lap and don't move again."

He released her, leaving white and red imprints of his grip on her throbbing wrist. Rae didn't move. She couldn't take a breath, couldn't do anything but pray a jumbled entreaty for her safety. . .or that she would at least die with dignity.

Five minutes later the car pulled into a crowded mall parking lot and stopped. "Remember—no police, no blabbing. Keep your nose where it belongs, and just maybe it will stay there—in one piece." He leaned across her, opened the door, and shoved her out. "We'll be watching you to make sure, Miss Prescott."

The door slammed in her face and the car left, weaving sedately out of the parking lot onto the main street.

Molly Ferguson, the music minister's wife, dropped her off at home twenty minutes later. She smilingly waved away Rae's stammering thanks, her plump face concerned but tactful. "If you change your mind and need to talk—give us a call, okay?"

"Thanks, Molly." Rae forced her voice to calmness, but didn't look across at her friend. Otherwise she would have started bawling like a heedless infant.

Caleb was waiting on the front porch. So, Rae saw with resignation, was Karen. She might have known her friend would use the opportunity to meet the man she insisted on calling Rae's date.

She clutched her purse and hurried up the brick walk toward them. It was fifteen minutes past the time for her dinner date, and Caleb's expression, while not impatient, was nonetheless questioning. Karen waved, her fire-engine red poncho practically glowing in the gathering dusk.

"It's a good thing you called me, honey. When I got here Caleb was ready to send for the cavalry or whatever 'cause you weren't here." She flashed Caleb a beguiling grin and poked him in the ribs with her elbow before turning back to Rae. "Where did you say your car was?"

Rae forced a smile. "Thanks, Karen. You can go back to the restaurant now. I'll tell you all about it later." Her eyes spoke eloquently, and Karen's brows lifted.

"By all means, excuse me, honey. Three's a crowd and all that. . . ." She blew Caleb a kiss. "Nice chattin' with you—ya'll come on down if you want decent food instead of—"

"Karen!"

"I'm going! I'm going!"

After she trotted laughingly down the walk and crossed the street, Rae gathered her courage and looked up at Caleb.

"I'm sorry I'm late." She lifted her chin. If Caleb pressed for an explanation, Rae was petrified of the consequences. She couldn't tell him the truth. Her home—and her life—would be in jeopardy. Yet she didn't want to lie, either.

It was difficult to read Caleb's expression in the diffuse yellow porchlight she had mercifully turned on before her 'trip.' He wasn't angry, but something hovered behind the lightly smiling eyes, something watchful, waiting. He glanced around as if searching the shadows, then put a hand under her elbow.

"Do you need to freshen up before we go?"

Rae stared blankly at him for a split second. "Ah, yes," she finally muttered. "I—I do need to freshen up." She gestured awkwardly to her three-year old suit. The cashmere sweater underneath itched with trickles of perspiration.

She was both relieved and unnerved by Caleb's perception. On the one hand, it provided an excuse that would give her a few more minutes to recover. But she had a gnawing suspicion he was not as relaxed as he seemed.

There was a pause, then Caleb said easily, "All right, Rae.

56

Take your time."

The suspicion grew that he was holding something back, but whether it was words of irritation or interrogation Rae did not know. At the moment she didn't have the strength for either. *If I lose control now, I might as well go sign my own death certificate. . . . Are they watching even now as we stand out here in full view?*

Ten minutes later, wearing the same suit but a fresh blouse, she was buckled snugly in the car beside Caleb. Her hands lay with deceptive calmness in her lap. If only her stomach didn't feel like it was doing cartwheels over her heart.

They ate dinner at the Sunbird, and Caleb kept up a light, non-threatening conversation that did not include any mention of her father, Rae's past, or the Starseeker case. Rae was almost relaxed when they left, gazing idly at the passing traffic and stores while she listened to Caleb relate a funny story about his cat, Sheba.

Then the car pulled into a side street and stopped.

"Tell me what happened this afternoon." Though spoken quietly, the words framed an order, not a request.

Rae threw him one apprehensive glance. "I don't want to talk about it." She clamped her jaw shut and turned her head away. Her throat muscles quivered as if they were stretched on a rack.

"Rae. . .what happened? Talk to me. Trust me—" He reached over and gently wrapped his fingers around her wrist. She gasped with pain. Caleb released her instantly. "What is it?"

"I—my wrist. I sprained it."

"How?"

She was trapped. She would either have to lie—or tell the truth. If she lied he would know it, not only because she was lousy at it, but because Caleb Myers was not a stupid man.

But if she told the truth, she could end up dead. Whatever else had happened this afternoon, she knew the two men were killers.

CHAPTER 11

She took a deep breath. "I really can't talk about it, Caleb. Please don't ask."

"Are you in trouble?"

Not as much as I would be if I told you I was. . . . "What would you call all the things that have happened to me in the last few weeks?" she snapped pettishly, feeling cornered. "Not to mention finding out my father is a crook—and Det. Grabowski all but accusing me of being in cahoots."

Her control fraying like an overstrained piece of rope, she found it impossible to stem the tumbling words once they started. "You sweet-talk me into going out to eat by promising to tell me about my father, but you haven't said a word!"

"Mmm. . ." In the muted glow of the dash lights, she thought she saw him smile. "I guess you do need to be filled in."

His hands slid idly up and down the steering wheel. "I hoped enjoying a nice quiet meal would relax you a little, help you get to know me better." He stared at his hands a minute, then finished evenly, "I can see that didn't work, so I'll tell you everything I can about your father and see if that will help."

He paused as if deep in thought, then irritably shrugged his shoulders. "Your father was last arrested in San Francisco five years ago. The charge was passing stolen goods. He jumped bond, hasn't been seen since." He watched her, gauging her reaction. "Do you remember him at all, Rae?"

"I remember an impression of long hair and some kind of jacket with a fringe. The fringe tickled me and I giggled. That's all. My mother—" she hesitated, then finished flatly, "—my mother was a drug addict. She had just enough sense to bring us here. She died a year later."

"Do you remember the police coming to talk to your uncle

once? You would have been about ten."

She shook her head. The pain was terrible.

"Don't look like that. Your parents' lifestyle doesn't affect the person you are." His calm perception healed, sustained, and Rae relaxed a little.

"I know. When I accepted Christ, I realized that. My best friend in high school had been explaining it for months. I never understood until Christ—" she fumbled for words, spread her hands, "—until He just sort of filled me up with His love. I really did feel washed clean, a new creature. I've truly accepted my parents, my past. But—"

"But now it's rearing up like a fire-breathing dragon and trying to take a big bite out of you, huh?"

"Well. . .at least breathe its fiery bad breath on me." They smiled at each other, and Caleb's hand moved as if he were about to touch her face, but then dropped back onto the seat.

"Rae, I can't tell you too much about the case—but I promise you when I have more definitive information about your father, I'll let you know."

"Can you tell me anything about what's going on?"

There was a longer pause this time, and he bowed his head as if in prayer. Then he turned to Rae, and his eyes were very clear, almost glowing in the night. "I can tell you only that the danger is real, and it could become even more dangerous than you've already experienced. I think an organization known as IOS is involved. It's not organized crime, but they're still deadly."

"I-OS?"

His voice grim, Caleb explained. "It started as a bunch of renegade businessmen—powerful, executive-type men who had either been fired or laid off. For revenge they got together and started sabotaging their companies—stealing information or technology and selling to rival corporations, manipulating stock. . .at first it was mostly white-collar crime. But this is the third time in three years I've been on a case involving them. They used to steer clear of anything involving the military.

Security is so tight it's not worth the effort."

"What happened?"

"We're not quite sure, but about four years ago we think there was a major change in policy. Things started getting nasty—a couple of deaths by mysterious causes, some arson, a case or two of blackmail. The members apparently got carried away by their power."

"Is there one particular man in charge?"

"Again, we're not sure. The whole organization is so loosely structured, the secrecy so well-maintained, that we don't have a lot to go on. A name dropped here, a letter there—every now and then some sketchy tidbit from a snitch. . . ."

Rae rolled the name around her tongue a few times, feeling the insidious threat in the two deadly syllables, even in the safety of Caleb's car. "It's a strange name. Does it mean something?"

He gave her an approving look that was mixed with gravity. "That was quick of you. Whoever came up with it has a brilliant mind, but a twisted sense of humor. It's a Greek word, and the simplest translation is poison, a corrosive, destructive kind of poison."

Rae shuddered.

As if sensing her fear, Caleb suddenly slid over. His hand came down on her shoulder. "Rae, they're dangerous. They don't care anymore about simple revenge—they're after power as well. Power, money, revenge. . .some of Satan's favorite tools."

Greater is he. . . , Rae thought. She shivered again, and Caleb's warm hand slid behind her neck. He massaged the rigid tendons, and Rae almost gasped at the sensations. She had never felt like this before, all jumpy and sizzling on the outside, and melting like hot caramel inside. She wanted him to take his hand away, but she wanted the feeling never to stop.

"I need to go home," she said.

"In a minute." The hand slid to her chin and gently turned it toward him. "Rae, I know you're hiding something from me. Are you sure you won't tell me what it is?"

60

Mutely she shook her head. Pulling away, she folded in on herself, clutching her elbows. There was no way Caleb Myers could protect her twenty-four hours a day. "I'm fine."

"I don't believe you. You've been nervous, even frightened all evening. You knocked over your water glass, spilled pie in your lap, and every time you look at me I want to take you in my arms." He ignored her startled jump. "Believe me, it's not a feeling I'm comfortable with either. You're wrecking my concentration, little cat's claw."

"You're not doing much for me, either."

With a chuckle he moved back to his side of the car. Neither of them spoke as he drove Rae home.

As they pulled up in the drive Caleb said, "I'll check out your house." Rae could tell from the determination in his jutting jaw that she might as well not protest. "Stay behind me."

He led her up the back porch stairs and took her key. His body hummed with alertness and tension. Instructing Rae to stay by the door, he searched the back rooms swiftly, silently. He looked threatening, but he also looked as capable of protecting her as a sword-wielding archangel.

"You can check to see if anything is missing. I don't see any signs of forced entry, though," Caleb announced in a normal voice a few minutes later.

Rae opened her mouth to tell him about the missing pieces of sheet music, then closed it. She wandered obediently around her living quarters and the store, but everything was in its proper place. Except—

She couldn't prevent the dismayed, clumsy gesture of her arm. Caleb was beside her instantly. "The quarter note there—" she pointed to the shiny brass note mounted on a marble stand, "—and that music box. They've been moved."

"How can you tell? The police could have—"

"No." Her voice was firm. "I have everything in a specific position—I moved them all back after the police left." She met his gaze with a blend of self-consciousness and stubborn certainty. "I'm like that with these—until he died, my uncle gave me a different one for every birthday since I was eight years old. I can always tell when someone has picked them up."

"Hmm." There was lurking amusement behind the watchfulness. "I see."

He spent thirty minutes checking the store for signs of forced entry, wiretaps on her phone, and concealed listening devices. There were none. He called someone on the phone, his voice soft but persuasive, then told Rae that an extra team would be detailed to watch the Prescott mansion.

As he left, he touched Rae's bruised cheek. "Something is going on here, and until we know what it is—" He stuffed his hands casually in the pockets of his pleated wool slacks, "—be careful. Independence can be taken to extremes, you know."

Two blocks from Rae's house, Caleb pulled over to the curb. After locking the car, he loped back down the street, keeping in the shadows and dodging streetlamps. The two men on station in the second story of the vacant house told him everything was quiet. They had seen nothing, and no one had tried to enter Rae's house. Radio contact with two other under-cover men confirmed the report. Caleb sympathized with their frustration and boredom. He had a feeling, however, that it wouldn't last much longer.

Rae's living quarters might be comfortably cluttered, but she was meticulous about every aspect of Joyful Noise. If she claimed those two objects had been moved, Caleb believed her. The nagging question was—why?

And the other nagging question—what had happened to her before he arrived to take her to dinner?

CHAPTER 12

During the next week, Rae stayed on edge, the joyfulness of Easter eluding her. The Easter cantata was declared a success, but Rae shrugged aside the compliments she received for her accompaniment. She and the Lord knew who had been responsible for the brilliance of her playing. Rae's mind had been elsewhere.

She had not seen the bogus detective, or his henchman, since the day they took her for a drive. But she felt their presence everywhere, even if she couldn't prove it. Her skin seemed to crawl permanently from the sensation of being watched.

Caleb had stopped by twice. The last time he told her he had to go out of town for a few days to check some leads. He didn't say what leads. He had promised to be back by Friday, which was yesterday now. He hadn't called or come by, however. Rae tried not to dwell on the implications of that.

There hadn't been a lot of customers. Rae used the free time to catch up on her bookkeeping, and devote more time to her students. A lady who was teaching herself piano dropped by twice to purchase more music, and the balding man with thick-lensed glassed who collected old sheet music stopped by again. This time he stayed to converse a little nervously with Rae.

"I wondered if you would mind if I just rummaged through your music," he asked, mopping his balding head with a folded handkerchief.

Rae wondered why he was sweating. It was twenty-four degrees outside, and the radiators dotting the store were unable to pull the indoor temperature much above sixty-eight. "Well ..." she hesitated. In her experience, customers who wanted to "just look" ended up creating more work for Rae—and no revenues.

"I won't make a mess," he promised anxiously.

He made Rae feel petty. She smiled. "Go ahead. Let me know if you need any help."

One of her favorite piano students arrived about then, and Rae forgot about the stoop-shouldered man. He was gone the next time she checked.

The raspy-voiced woman who thought "Ode to Joy" was from Beethoven's Fifth stopped by the next afternoon. "I'm looking for a piece of religious music," she said. "It's called 'The Lord is My Light and My Salvation.' Do you have it?"

"I certainly do," Rae replied. "That's one of my favorites."

The woman did not look impressed. She coughed as she followed Rae, her eyes darting everywhere. After paying for the music, she hurried out of the store without so much as a thank you.

Rae decided to drop the mix-up over Beethoven. Such a strange, almost ill-tempered woman would undoubtedly not take to correction kindly. But she didn't seem the type to want religious music either.

Rae was writing the entry in her log book when the bell tinkled and a man wearing the uniform of the phone company sauntered in.

"Got a report that your phone's out of order," he announced.

Rae reached for the phone under the counter. She listened to the dial tone and looked at the man. "There's nothing wrong with my phone. You must have the wrong address."

The man scowled. "This place is Joyful Noise, ain't it? Well, I got orders to check your phones."

Rae shivered suddenly. "Orders from who?"

"The President of the U.S.," he replied sardonically. "What kind of dumb question is that, lady? Orders from the phone company, okay?"

Rae was afraid, but she didn't know why. He might just be a rude, uncouth serviceman. On the other hand. . . . "Why don't you tell me the name of your boss and let me call and confirm the order?" She reached casually for the phone.

He gave her a thoroughly disgusted look. "You want to check my fingerprints, too? Forget it, lady. I got too many other calls to waste time waiting on you." He picked up the metal toolbox he had dumped on the floor. "Don't blame me when your phone won't work."

Well, Rae thought after he stomped out the door, *so much for courteous, friendly service.* But she was still glad she hadn't backed down. She started to call the phone company, but a customer entered the store, and the moment passed.

Something woke her that night. She lay in bed, head pressed into the pillow, eyes stretched wide as she stayed rigidly still, listening. There it was again—the creaking of a floorboard somewhere up front.

The crawling sensation singed her spine, and for a moment she was afraid she was going to be ill. Then she was angry.

She tossed back the covers and snatched on her robe over her floor length silk gown. Grabbing the poker by the bed, she tiptoed out into the hall. The door to the store was still locked, but even through the thick oak panels she could hear the faint shuffling sound.

She lifted the poker. "Get out of here!" she yelled. "I'm calling the po-" She stopped. She had been warned not to call the police.

From the other side of the door came the muffled sound of clanging tools and scrambling footsteps. They thudded across the floor—away from Rae—and she heard the painful screech from one of the windows. Unopened since summer, they were stiff from disuse.

Then there was silence.

Rae's arms flopped down to her sides. Her fingers were so nerveless she almost dropped the poker. Shivering, she staggered into the kitchen and put on the kettle. Then she sat down, flipped her braid back over her shoulder, and tried to figure out what to do.

After a few minutes she went to the bedroom and looked in her purse. Caleb Myers wasn't police, exactly, and he had given her his card, writing the number of the motel where he was staying on the back. It was two o'clock in the morning. Was he there? If he was, how would he react to being awakened out of a sound sleep? She knew how *she* would react.

The kettle was whistling. The merry, homey sound dragged across her nerves. She turned off the gas and stood at the stove. The heat warmed her chilled hands, and she held them over the burner. Her mouth twisted because she couldn't keep them still.

Caleb had more or less told her she was too independent. *All right, Mr. DSA Agent Myers, let's see how you react when someone disturbs you unexpectedly.* She dialed the number and asked the sleepy clerk to connect her with room 117.

He answered on the second ring. "Myers."

"Caleb?"

"Rae? Is that you? What's the matter? Your voice is trembling."

He was alert, the calm voice concerned.

"I hate to bother you, but—" she chewed on her lip, then confessed hurriedly, "someone broke into the store again. Can you—"

"Where are you calling from?"

"The kitchen. He ran—"

"Stay there. Turn on all the lights. I'll be there in five minutes. Did you call the police?"

"No!" Her voice was too sharp. She tried to modify it. "I don't want to call the police. I can't. They said. . . ." She stopped, but it was too late.

"Who said?" Caleb repeated quietly.

"N—nothing. I meant—I—"

"Don't move. I'll be there in five minutes." He paused, then added, "If you have hot chocolate, I'd rather have that than tea."

She opened the door after his voice softly called out her name, and she recognized the calm, crisp tones. He looked so strong, so capable, that she fought the urge to throw herself in his arms.

Her face must have revealed her chaotic feelings. He smiled crookedly and opened his arms wide. "Come here," he prompted.

She took a step, then stopped, stiffening her shoulders. "I'm fine."

They went in to the kitchen, and Rae explained what happened, then followed Caleb into the store. He poked around carefully, his face revealing nothing. Finally, he turned to Rae and gestured for her to go back to the kitchen.

"Your phone has been tapped," he said. "Is the one back here on the same line as the store?"

She nodded slowly. "An extra line costs too much." Her voice wobbled. "I sound like a broken record, don't I? Actually, the Lord has lived up to His promise about providing, because I have a roof over my head, food to eat, and can pay all my bills. I hope you—"

"Rae—" His hand moved to the pager at his side, then stopped. He cast a swift, measuring glance over Rae. "I have to leave you for a few minutes," he told her, his voice calm, matter-of-fact. "Stay here, in the kitchen, and drink your tea. Can you do that for me?"

He lifted his hand, but he must have seen something in her face because he dropped it back by his side. Something like a wince passed through his eyes.

"Where are you going?" Rae was proud of her own matter-of-fact voice.

He smiled, an infuriating smile that warned Rae he wasn't going to answer her. "I'll be back as soon as I can," he repeated.

Rae's chin lifted. "I'm perfectly all right," she promised frigidly. "You can go play all the spy games you want without fear that I'll dissolve into a gibbering idiot. If I can handle being—" She stopped. She was perilously close to the gibbering idiot label.

This time Caleb didn't ignore her. His hand urged her over and pressed her down on the trestle bench. "All right, Rae." He was very calm, but firm. "Tell me what's happened. And don't try to fob me off with evasions, or try to come up with a plausible lie." He looked at her. "You're lousy at it, as I expect you know."

"I wouldn't be much of a Christian if I was good at it, would I?" Rae startled herself by smiling ruefully. Being with Caleb made her feel incredibly brave. "I've probably behaved stupidly, but then I'm not used to being held at gunpoint."

"What?" All the color left his face. For once the imperturbable Caleb Myers looked completely knocked off balance. Rae felt a brief sting of satisfaction that she instantly quelled.

"Last week." She explained the whole story calmly. "I was too frightened to think properly. I'd do anything to keep someone from burning or trashing my home. It's all I have. It's been a week since it happened, and until a few minutes ago I was hoping. . . ." Her hands lifted in a futile gesture. "Have you or the others had any leads?"

"Not until now." His voice was grim. "I trust this time you have a fair idea of what they look like. I'll ask Grabowski to set up a photo line-up at their Detective Bureau. Can you describe the car?"

"It was a—a car." She blushed when Caleb groaned. "I'm sorry. I just never notice things like that much. About all I can tell you is that it reminded me of the kind of car all you undercover types seem to prefer."

Caleb shook his head and tugged on the errant lock of hair dangling over his forehead. "Rae, why didn't you tell me when this happened?"

She didn't want to look at him. "I couldn't. I should have, but at the time I just couldn't." Ashamed of her fear, and the remnants of cowardice that made her avoid facing Caleb, Rae lifted her head. Her toes curled up inside her slippers, and her fingers twined together in her lap in a death grip. But she met the rebuke unflinchingly.

His face softened. "All right. I understand. But we're calling the police in now." He tilted his head and studied her somberly. The call she made to him had been brief, but potentially dangerous. Would IOS investigate, or assume he was just a male friend? "What would you have done if I hadn't been in the motel when you called?"

She quivered as if he had struck her. "I don't know. . . ." Her chin lifted. "But I would have managed."

The tender look that glimmered in his golden eyes turned her poker of a spine to flimsy straw. "I imagine you would," he murmured. His finger touched the end of her nose. "Don't move. I'll be back as soon as I can."

CHAPTER 13

He ran lightly, soundlessly across the street, slipping in and out of shadows with automatic caution. The two FBI men were as steamed—and perturbed—as Caleb. They notified Grabowski, and everyone converged minutes later at Rae's back porch.

Caleb watched her greet everyone with resigned aplomb. She had combed her hair and twisted it up, and was dressed in a soft pink warm-up suit. Her arms and legs still jutted out all over the place, swinging awkwardly as she led them down the narrow winding hall to the store. She watched, gray eyes still and dark, while Caleb pointed out the nasty, unobtrusive induction coil planted under the counter. Even when he described her brief abduction by car she didn't stir.

Grabowski looked as if he had been sleeping in his clothes. He was scowling, irritable, and short-tempered. Caleb's voice smoothed out and softened accordingly as he explained the circumstances, and thanked the detective for his help and cooperation. He did not dwell on the difficulty of maintaining a surveillance over a structure with as many angles and sides as the Prescott mansion.

He didn't try to absolve himself or the FBI from blame, either. Grabowski's surliness flattened out a little. He questioned Rae with surprising patience.

They fought a brief but furious battle over whether or not to leave the bug in place. Thanks to Rae, Grabowski won.

Elbows akimbo, with her fists bunched on either side of her waist, she stubbornly refused to listen to Caleb at all. "I'm already in danger—and I don't see how I could possibly be more terrified than I was that afternoon," she pointed out with what Caleb decided was mule-headed naivete. "If they find out that—that *thing's* gone, they'll know for sure I called the police."

Her gaze bounced off Caleb's, and he watched her hands move in restless patterns until she clenched them behind her back. "Being threatened was bad enough, but what if they drive by one night and chuck a molotov cocktail through the window?"

"It wouldn't only be the Prescott mansion that suffered," Caleb pointed out evenly. If he hadn't been so concerned, he would have smiled at Rae's stubbornness. She might be innocent to the sharks of the world, but she definitely wasn't the kind of woman who buckled beneath adversity.

Rae tossed her head. "I'll just make sure I don't conduct any incriminating conversations over the phone. Maybe those guys will even learn something about music."

She stood by the cash register, looking defiant and pale. Even with the bruises faded now to an unbecoming green and yellow, Caleb discovered that he wanted to haul her into his arms and kiss those ugly bruises, then her eyes, her mouth. The strength of his emotions amazed and appalled him.

A fresh-faced man with a shock of carrot red hair approached. He spoke to Grabowski. "Rest of the place is clean, sir. But it looks like Miss Prescott probably interrupted a second placement." He glanced at Rae. "They were going to put it inside one of the music boxes."

Rae's body jerked, and her determination faltered. "Another one?" Her voice rose and Caleb moved to her side. She turned to Grabowski. "Why are they doing this? Why?"

Her hands flew out from behind her back, fluttering awkwardly. The long slender fingers, Caleb noted with sudden tenderness, ended in short and practically nonexistent nails. He had a feeling she was a wonderfully gifted musician, even if she was sublimely unaware of the rest of the world.

Unfortunately, the world seemed determined to rattle her cage, and as her control disintegrated, Caleb prayed to be there when she fell apart.

"Do you still think my father's involved?" she was asking.

71

"Am *I* still under suspicion?"

"Miss Prescott. . ." Grabowski began awkwardly, looking uncomfortable.

"I've told her about her father—and I've also told her about IOS." Caleb put his hand on Rae's shoulder. This time she didn't object, and he knew she was close to tears at last. Her eyes had a brilliant, glassy look.

He waited until he felt her relax a little. "Rae, have any of your customers acted strangely, made unusual requests—looked suspicious? Anything? Think before you answer—and don't leave something out because you think it's silly or irrelevant."

He shot Grabowski a look. Both men were aware that, while wire-tapping was a federal offense, the investigation for this incident still belonged to CSPD. He and the detective had met several times, however, and Grabowski was content to let Caleb handle Rae.

. . .For the time being, anyway. Caleb had a feeling that if he didn't find the discipline to harness all the turbulent emotion Rae seemed to generate in him, Grabowski might quit being so amenable.

Rae was shaking her head and chewing her bottom lip. "Business has been slow," she said.

Her hair, so hastily pinned, was starting to slip. Caleb couldn't help it. His fingers moved up to push the pins back in place. Thick and soft, the shining strands smelled like lavender potpourri and fresh linens. So much for detachment.

Rae took a step away. He dropped his hands. "About the only thing I remember," she mused, faint color washing across the bridge of her nose, "is a woman who wanted Beethoven's 'Ode to Joy' but she got the symphonies mixed up—wait."

She hesitated. Grabowski shifted impatiently. Joe, one of the FBI men from across the street, started to say something. Caleb lifted an eyebrow, and Joe shut his mouth.

"What, Rae?" he asked after a minute, when he could tell she needed encouragement to share whatever the thought was.

"There is something. . ." she said slowly, "but it's so silly—" she looked startled, and grinned up at Caleb sheepishly. "But like you said. . .after the first break-in, I did discover that all my copies of Beethoven's Fifth and Ninth symphonies were missing."

Grabowski looked disgusted, and Rae planted two small fists on her hips. "Well, it might be irrelevent to you, but it's *my* music, and *my* business."

"You probably misfiled them. After all the excitement you were probably pretty rattled."

The faint band of red deepened until two red coins dotted her cheeks. "Detective Grabowski," she stated frostily, "I may be a little—rattled—but *nothing* interferes with running my store. That music is not misplaced. It's missing."

Caleb dropped his hand over her right one, which was moving furiously up and down the counter. He was amused and relieved at the same time. This little kitten did have claws, and used them, however unwisely. Grabowski's face was turning just about as red as Rae's.

The man was inches away from giving Rae the rough side of his tongue. A crackerjack detective, he kept himself under iron control, and Caleb had seen that he expected the same from others. He definitely had little patience to tolerate Rae's flashfire temper.

Caleb fixed a serene but commanding gaze upon him. He did not look at Rae. After pressing her fingers one last time, he removed his hand. "We've determined that they must be using the store as a drop," he said, his voice pacifying. "It's the only explanation that makes sense."

He propped his hip on the edge of the counter and crossed his arms. "I think Fisher is our man. Joe and Charlie told me he came to the store again this past week, though he left empty-handed. He could have been leaving something behind."

"There's something else."

That was Charlie, a good-looking guy in his late twenties. He was staring at Rae with a brooding, calculating look that unaccountably irritated Caleb.

"Miss Prescott is being tailed," he announced flatly, glancing at Grabowski, "and not by us. Are they some of yours?"

Grabowski's eyes narrowed. "Describe him."

"Average height, slightly overweight. Dark hair, wears a blue and yellow ski jacket or a red plaid lumber jacket. Joe got a picture of him the other day. So far no I.D."

Grabowski muttered under his breath. "I haven't noticed anybody like that," Rae faltered.

"Why should you?" Caleb straightened, jerked his chin slightly and eyed the stairs. The two FBI men started toward them.

"There's nothing up there," Rae called after them in numb bewilderment as they reached the first landing. "Just boxes and some old furniture. I keep it closed."

"Relax, Rae," Caleb said, and she turned to gaze up at him with a heartbreaking blend of fear, puzzlement—and wonder. *Don't look at me like that, sweetheart. It makes me want all sorts of things I can't afford to ask you right now.* "It would be a good place to stash a few things, wouldn't it? When's the last time you went up there?"

"We checked it after the first break-in," Grabowski snapped. "It's clean."

Rae's mouth quirked. "It's hardly that. I bet there's three years' worth of dirt and dust all over everything." She examined her slipper-clad toes with elaborate concentration. "I keep meaning to go over everything at least once a year, but time sort of gets away from me."

Joe and Charlie returned a few minutes later, dusting their hands on their slacks and sneezing. Caleb and Grabowski met them at the bottom of the stairs and held a brief consultation. In a few minutes he returned to Rae.

"It's still—clean." His eyes twinkled briefly. "In one capacity, anyway." He gestured to the watching group of men. "We're going to give you a number to call in an emergency. It reaches the guys across the street—they had a modular phone set up. Hopefully, you'll feel a little safer."

Rae swallowed. Caleb tried to keep his face impassive. "Just remember, it's for emergencies only. If you can get to another phone to call, do so, since we're leaving the tap on your phone."

"That does make sense," she said slowly, after a minute. "What can I do to help?"

Go on an extended vacation, Caleb wanted to say but didn't. He had a feeling Rae's guardian angels would have to work double time to keep her from dashing her foot against a whole truckload of stones. "Just try to act normally. That means," he tapped her nose playfully, "that you continue to play the part of a musician, and leave the detective work to us."

Grabowski had other ideas. "It might help if you start keeping a written description of every customer. If one acts in any way peculiar, write that down as well." He glanced at Caleb, but this time did not back down. "And don't leave it lying around for anyone to find. Take it out of the store at night."

The phone rang, and Rae jumped violently. Caleb wrapped a protective arm around her shoulders. "Go ahead and answer it," he told her with an encouraging smile.

He felt her back straighten, saw her chin rise. The hand that reached out was as calm as the eye of a hurricane. Caleb's feelings were more like the hundred-and-twenty mile-an-hour winds.

"Hello?" The anxiety in her voice could not be disguised. After a second her eyes flew to Grabowski, and she began furiously chewing on her lip. "I'm fine, Nancy," she spoke with cheerful confidence. "I just thought I heard that prowler again, and they came to investigate. I'm sorry to cause such drama, but I promise everything's under control. Yes, I will. Thanks."

She hung up, staring at the phone as if it were a snake. Her gaze moved around the watching circle of men, stopping again on Grabowski. Caleb felt her, incredibly, lean into his chest almost as if seeking support. He tightened his arm, and rubbed his hand reassuringly over her shoulder.

He looked down at her, and Rae blushed. She seemed to realize all at once where she was and stiffened. Caleb dropped his arm, but could not resist winking at her. "You did pretty well for an unworldly musician, Miss Prescott. And without telling a lie, too."

The relief that flooded her face relaxed everyone in the room. The relief was short-lived, though, because Grabowski's pager suddenly squawked with crackling urgency.

"I'll be back," he said tersely, and left the room to go call in by radio.

When he returned a few minutes later, he surveyed everyone for a moment, his grim face looking gray with fatigue. "We found the unmarked car stolen from our inventory nine days ago. It's probably the one in which Miss Prescott was abducted. No clues. No prints. It's been wiped clean as a car on the showroom floor."

CHAPTER 14

"It won't look right. Everyone will think you and I—that you're—" Rae threw up her hands in exasperation. "Stop grinning at me like that! You know good and well what they'll think when you show up at choir practice with me and just sit."

Caleb looked infuriatingly indulgent. "I don't care if everyone does think that. In fact, I think it's an idea with a lot of merit."

Rae stomped around the store, locking the doors and turning the sign. "Don't be ridiculous. The whole church is resigned to my being a nice but eccentric old maid."

"*That's* what is ridiculous. What puzzles me is why some lucky man hasn't snatched you up a long time ago."

She began straightening music, not looking at him. "I haven't had time—and it's not exactly as though I'm Delilah enticing Samson."

He came up behind her so softly she didn't know he was there until she turned and ran into him. His hands balanced her, but didn't insist when she moved aside to the next bin. "Few men want a Delilah. Look what happened to Samson."

Determined to let him know she understood the real motivation behind his suitor-like attention, Rae quit straightening music and produced what she hoped was a sophisticated smile. "Caleb, it's all right. You're not going to hurt my vanity by keeping our relationship strictly professional. I know you and Det. Grabowski and Agent Ram—Rom—whatever his name is—I know you all think I need a bodyguard."

"This is not," Caleb replied calmly, "merely professional."

He subjected her to a lazy, masculine appraisal that completely flustered her.

77

"But I'm not even pretty," she blurted. "Caleb, you're embarrassing me." She lifted her hands in a sweeping gesture. "Look at me—my hair's a mess because I never take time to have it cut and styled. My nose is too long, my face is too pale. . .and even after all the ballet lessons Uncle Floyd insisted I take, I'm about as graceful as a goose. My brother used to call me Spiderlegs."

"I imagine a stockbroker wouldn't have much of an imagination," Caleb murmured, moving to stand in front of her again.

Rae froze. "How did you know my brother was a stockbroker?"

He hesitated, then revealed easily enough, "Part of the background check. With everything that's occurred involving the Prescotts, albeit indirectly, an investigation is standard procedure."

"Of all the sneaky. . .you could have at least warned me!" Outraged, hurt, she pushed by him. "I'm still a suspect, right? Because of my father! You don't want to protect me at all—you just want to—to *spy* on me! See if I have a contact at—at *church*."

It was always the same. Always. Just when she had started to trust. . . . "It might. even be the minister—or Jerry, the music director. I see him all the time, you know. Don't touch me!" She darted around the other side of the bins of music and glared. She wanted to crawl under the house and die. "If you think you can trot tamely off to church with me now—"

He had followed her, the golden eyes intent, determined. Rae thought about continuing the cat-and-mouse dodging, but she knew who would win in the end. She straightened to her full height and stood her ground. "And if you think you can bully—mmf—"

His hands tugged her into his embrace, and his mouth came down on hers. As a first kiss, it was extremely thorough. When he lifted his mouth at last, all she could do was stare into the brightness of his eyes.

"I've been wanting to do that since the night I rescued you, and you read me the riot act for not getting there sooner." His hands, those warm, strong hands, lifted and held her face. "You're beautiful where it counts, Rae—inside. And I'm not going to let anything or anyone defile what you are."

"You don't know me. . ." she whispered miserably. Her hands clung to his shoulders. He felt so good, so strong.

"I know more than you think." He nuzzled her nose. "And the reason I'm playing the part of bodyguard is because I want to." He smiled a little. "It would doubtless surprise you, my prickly little cat's claw, but half a dozen cops and agents were all vying for the honor." The smile broadened to quiet satisfaction. "I won."

His head lowered again. "And now, since I'm supposed to be your boyfriend. . .I need to practice my part a little more." He kissed her again.

If he "practiced" any better, Rae knew she would melt into a puddle on the floor. His lips breathed her name softly, as he cuddled her against his shoulder.

Rae wanted to cry from the sweetness of it. His tender touch ignited a flame in her. She was soaring, melting, caught up in a kind of music she had only been able to create through her hands before.

After awhile, in a warm gust of laughter, Caleb murmured against her mouth, "Don't you think you better finish in here? We're going to be late for choir practice."

Caleb became her shadow the next few weeks. Rae almost enjoyed the teasing and bantering at church, and Caleb took everything in stride.

But then, Caleb Myers took life that way. When he was with Rae, he treated her like a cherished possession, like a rare, original edition of music. But he was careful never to take advantage of her vulnerability, and at the first hint of withdrawal

79

on her part, he always backed off.

When he talked with fellow agents or the police, he switched into the role of professional agent like a swallow to a song. Rae was constantly amazed at the deference accorded him, especially since he was assigned to the case mainly as a consultant.

Rae stuggled to emulate his unruffled demeanor. For awhile she was successful. Two weeks passed without incident, and the whole situation assumed the overtones of a game.

On her walks to and from the Gibson Girl, she tried to pick out which strolling individual, which car, held Agent Ramirez's men who had been assigned to tail her—and which might be the IOS agents.

She found that was virtually impossible. The gaping tourist with his camera could be an IOS thug. . .or the middle-aged man strolling with apparent enjoyment down the street could have placed an illegal wire tap on her phone. It could even be a woman.

After two weeks, Rae quit pretending that she enjoyed playing cops and robbers. She focused on her store, her students, and her music, praying for peace of mind.

Caleb had to fly back to Chicago, then on the D.C. He didn't explain why, and after their good-bye kiss, Rae forgot to ask. While he was gone, on a bright April morning with the forsythias bursting in butter yellow blossoms, Agent Ramirez and an FBI man she had never met came to the store.

"Rob," she put an apologetic hand on the shoulder of her favorite piano student, "I need to talk to these two gentlemen in private." She hesitated. Rob was a gifted, intelligent senior who had arranged his schedule to have morning lessons so he could work after school. He was more than capable of watching over Joyful Noise a few minutes. "Would you mind staying in the store and taking care of any customers? I can't afford to leave it unattended."

"No worries, Rae. Take your time." He glanced out into the other room. "You're not in any trouble, are you? Those two dudes don't exactly look like they're dying to hear Beethoven or Bach."

"Everything's fine," Rae responded, hoping she sounded convincing.

She led the two men to her parlor. Knowing that they wore .357 revolvers beneath their suit jackets, she found herself wanting to giggle at the incongruity of such men in her comfortable, cluttered Victorian-looking living room. "Would you like some iced tea, a soda?"

"No thanks." Agent Ramirez did not smile at her like he usually did. The cola brown eyes were somber, watchful.

Rae glanced at the other man. He was taller, lanky, with a hard face and lighter brown eyes flicking around the room.

"Is something wrong?" she asked into the growing silence.

"Miss Prescott. . ." Agent Ramirez said slowly, his voice that of the detached professional, "can you explain who is responsible for the monthly payments you've received in a Denver bank during the last three years?"

He might as well have accused her of heresy. "I—what?" She gaped at both men. "Monthly payments?"

"That's right," the other man confirmed. His low voice, a gravelly bass, trod over her nerves with hobnailed boots. "One thousand dollars a month to be exact. Deposited in a high interest yielding savings account for Rae M. Prescott."

"You have a nice little pile accumulated," Ramirez observed gently. "More than enough to negate all the claims you've made about lack of accessible cash. The account—" he finished, "has a non-penalty withdrawal after the first year."

With the suddenness of a deflated balloon, Rae collapsed awkwardly into the overstuffed easy chair that had been Uncle Floyd's favorite. "I don't know about any money," she looked down at her knees. The three-year old nubby silk designer skirt had a snag.

Her whole life had hit a snag. "I have no idea what account

81

you're talking about," she repeated, and pressed her lips tightly together.

"Miss Prescott, I know Caleb has warned you that IOS is a ruthless, amoral organization. If they've managed to trap you some way—blackmail, threats of physical violence—you're not going to be safe by keeping your mouth shut."

The tall man stepped over to the chair and stared down at her. "Are you aware of the possible penalties for committing crimes against the United States Government?" he asked. "The Starseeker program out at Falcon is considered a prototype. The sabotage of it has made a lot of people very angry."

He folded his arms across his chest, then finished with a deliberate indifference that froze her blood, "How would you like to spend the rest of your life in a federal prison, Miss Prescott?"

CHAPTER 15

Jackson Overstreet sat back in his chair and crossed his legs. His heavy jowls and broad forehead gave him the look of an aging bulldog. Right now, the lines creasing his face were even deeper than normal.

"You can't be sure you didn't blow your cover a month ago—and *that's* why the whole thing has bogged down, Cal." There was a pause, then he bit out, "In all the years I've known you, you've never allowed emotions to run your investigations before. I appreciate the FBI calling you in, but I'm not too happy right now, as you may have gathered. Polaris stands to lose more than just money."

Caleb was looking over the Chicago skyline, hands clasped behind his back. He turned around to face Jack. "I know," he admitted. "But I'm not going to apologize. Top secret investigation or not, I was not about to be a pharisaical witness to the assault and possible death of an innocent young woman." He watched a commercial jetliner climb until it disappeared in a cloud, then explained with careful neutrality, "Tray and I talked about this to some extent, and we both agreed that being her boyfriend is a lot easier cover than having a plainclothesman tagging along after her. Which, by the way, is the procedure when I'm not available."

Jack's hands slammed down on the desk. "Well, now, isn't that convenient? That really makes me happy! And when your *pretended* relationship ends up blinding you to the facts—what are you going to do then?"

Caleb eyed his friend calmly. "I'm going to continue to do the best job I can—regardless of the facts." He steepled his fingers, deliberately prolonging the pause. "And regardless of whatever mine and Rae's relationship might be. I want the truth, Jack, no matter how painful it is for me personally."

Overstreet slumped back and sighed, the tension easing from his shoulders. "I know." His mouth flickered. "I'm sorry, Cal. I guess this whole mess is getting to me more than I realized." The twitching smile reappeared briefly. "Your personal feelings notwithstanding. Her father's been on the FBI's wanted list for eighteen years, and now you tell me she's been having monthly deposits made in a Denver bank for the past three years."

Caleb idly toyed with his watchband. "Rae hasn't heard from her father since she was four. He deserted his wife, Rae, and Rae's older brother. I haven't learned all the details yet, but apparently Prescott and his wife were some of the earliest of the sixties hippies. I can understand Rae's reluctance to discuss her background."

He quit fiddling with his watch. "I haven't confronted her about the money yet—Tray just called me this morning."

"It's a little too much to be circumstantial, Cal." Overstreet hesitated, then asked bluntly, "Is there a chance you might have to take yourself off the case?"

"No." Caleb strolled back over and dropped down in one of the leather chairs across from his friend. "I'm convinced the evidence is just that—circumstantial. Rae Prescott is innocent."

"I don't see how you—"

"I say that because I've gotten to know her; I've watched her. She's a Christian. She lives her faith, which means there is no way she'd intentionally involve herself in something illegal."

Jack emitted a rude noise.

Caleb leaned across the desk to stare directly into the other man's skeptical eyes. "Jack, we've known each other for fifteen years. Do you think I could do something like that?"

He waited, and after an uncomfortable pause Jack reluctantly admitted, "You're the most honest, ethical man I know. That's why I backed down earlier. And I know you claim the quality of your lifestyle is because you're a Christian. But—"

"Forget the buts. I'm staking my professional reputation as

well as my personal feelings on this, my friend. Rae is innocent, a pawn. I'm pretty sure her father is behind it, but his daughter needs our help—not our harassment. Give me a little more time, okay? This case has more sides to it than a prism. I'm hoping to find out more about Rae's father when I fly to Washington."

Overstreet picked up a gold pen and twirled it irritably. "All right, Cal, I won't beat the horse to death. Go on—get out of here. Keep me posted on what you find out in D.C." He smiled, a real smile this time. "And good luck in the Springs."

Caleb stopped by his apartment long enough to check the mail and Sheba, who was comfortably entrenched in the manager's apartment. Then he packed some more clothes, flew to Washington and spent two days with a liaison agent poring over mountainous files at FBI headquarters. The morning of the third day, he flew back to Colorado Springs.

After meeting with Tray, Admiral Vale, and Archie Cohen, he checked into a new motel, then drove to Joyful Noise, his mind straying to the memory of the honesty, the shy wonder in a pair of gray eyes the color of morning mist after rain. He also had to acknowledge his anxiety at seeing them again; the conversation with Tray had not been pleasant.

It was a little before five on a cool, windy Friday afternoon; as he maneuvered through the heavy afternoon traffic, he wondered what his reception would be.

Joyful Noise was closed.

Thanking God for his photographic memory, Caleb prayed silently as he located the nearest public phone and dialed the agents stationed across the street from Rae's house. He knew Rae had given permission for the FBI to put their own tap on her phone.

"This is Myers. What's up? The store is closed."

"She got a call about some old sheet music—Broadway show tunes, I think. The old lady was leaving town in the morning, so

Miss Prescott closed up early to go pick up the stuff."

"Who went with her?"

"J.W. and MacArthur from the Springs intelligence unit are tailing her. She refused to wait for Chuck to go with her in her car." Joe's voice plainly revealed what he thought about that.

"What was the address?" Caleb was not used to feeling this kind of fear. A metallic taste trickled down his throat, soured his clenched stomach. "When did she leave?"

The agent played the tape back. A scratchy, quavering voice directed Rae to a house in southwest Colorado Springs. Caleb told Joe he'd be back in touch, and to check with Grabowski. After hanging up, he borrowed a city map from the convenience store clerk, pinpointed the address, and the route Rae would have taken.

"You need to buy it?" the clerk asked.

"No." He almost grinned. "I won't be needing it now."

The traffic was appalling—slow, irritating, noisy. Caleb forced himself to maintain his equanimity. Grabowski's men were tailing her; it was an old lady's voice. . .it couldn't be a trap.

He turned off onto a narrow two-lane street, his muscles relaxing a little when the traffic finally thinned. A few minutes later he turned again onto the street where the elderly woman lived. Eighty-year-old trees lined cracked sidewalks and shaded the small but stately looking older homes.

Several cars were parked on either side, all of them older but well-kept models—except for a sheepish looking mud-splattered Volkswagen bug parked halfway down the block. Caleb drove past, his mouth softening briefly as his eye caught the shiny black quarter note painted on the door.

He pulled into a driveway four houses down, then casually reversed back into the street. Grabowski's men waited in a medium blue sedan parked inconspicuously next to the drive where Caleb had turned around. They exchanged brief glances, then Caleb pulled over to the curb and parked across the street from Rae's car. After turning off the engine, he slouched down in the car seat, looking as if he might be settling down for a catnap. Nothing was further from the truth.

Several minutes passed, and only two cars went by. Caleb automatically noted the model and color, even as he kept his gaze trained on the house where Rae had apparently gone. Another car went by. Suddenly, Caleb sat up and glanced behind him. That chocolate brown Chevy had gone by not two minutes earlier, traveling the other way.

Movement across the street jerked his head back around. Rae was coming out of the house, her hands clutching a large manila envelope, face smiling down at a short, tottering older lady. Rae waved good-bye, then walked down the slate path to her car.

From down the street there came the sound of a car engine revving. The Chevy hurtled toward Rae like a deadly avalanche as she fumbled obliviously with the lock to her car door.

Caleb shot out of his car and sprinted across the street.

Tires squealed and hot wind blew over him as he grabbed Rae around her waist and hurled both of them over the sloped hood of the VW. As they knocked against the metal and then tumbled down into the gutter, Caleb heard tires squeal again as the car disappeared around the corner.

His ear also caught the sound of running footsteps, and he rolled swiftly, shielding Rae with his body. The two plain-clothesmen skidded to a halt, faces pale.

"Are you all right?" J.W. asked while MacArthur spoke urgently into his radio.

Caleb nodded shortly and turned to Rae. She was still clutching the manila envelope to her chest, and the backs of her hands were scraped raw, oozing. Her eyes were blank with shock. Caleb lifted her in his arms. "It's all right, Rae," he murmured. Carrying her across to his car, he waited while J.W. opened the back door, then set her gently on the seat. "Let's see what you've got besides scraped hands."

"My knees and my right elbow," Rae replied calmly. She tried to smile. "I'm a popular punching bag for those guys, aren't I?"

She stared from Caleb to the detective, then back at Caleb. "It *was* IOS, wasn't it?"

J.W. glanced at Caleb, cleared his throat. "Miss Prescott, do you need medical treatment?"

Rae glared at both men. "You're not going to tell me, right? Fine." She shoved at Caleb, who was crouched at her feet in the open car door. "Thanks for rescuing me again, Mr. Special Agent. Send me a bill."

"Rae, sit here a minute until you've recovered."

"I'm not hurt—and I want to go home. I've got some music to catalog." She thrust the manila envelope in front of Caleb's nose. "Broadway show tunes—classics. *South Pacific, Oklahoma*...they're all in the original covers. I hope they're okay. . . ."

She started to open the envelope, and Caleb covered her injured hands with one of his. "Rae—honey. Relax. You're safe."

"Did she hit her head?"

Caleb examined the woman sitting rigidly in front of him. Her eyes were wide and strained, still staring blankly. There was a smudge of dirt across one cheek, and some of the pins holding her hair up had fallen, allowing one of the braids to slip over her ear. But Caleb did not see any overt signs of a head injury.

He released her hands, lifting his to her head. With gentle fingers he probed the heavy, silken layers, freeing more pins until the whole mass tumbled across his forearms.

"Now look what you've done," Rae snapped. "It takes *hours* to fix it right." She drew a shallow, quivering breath. "Caleb, I'm really glad to see you, but I want you to leave me alone for a minute. Please."

Caleb sighed. Standing, he motioned to the detective, and they walked to the front of the car. "She doesn't want us to see her break down," he informed the puzzled man wryly. He watched as Evan McArthur approached, the normally pleasant black face wearing an intimidating scowl. "Did you get the license number radioed in?"

"I could only make out the first three numbers," Evan bit out savagely.

"That's okay—I got it." Caleb ignored Evan's astonishment and reeled off the number.

He had never felt quite so frustrated in his life. He knew they couldn't blow their cover by pursuing the car, especially if there was a chance the incident had been designed just to frighten— not kill—Rae. But how many times would the intent be to frighten if Caleb kept coming to her rescue? The thought was not a pleasant one.

"I know how you feel, Myers," J.W. offered sympathetically. "This case is one big headache. We tail her for protection, but we can't follow up on a lead because we can't afford to let IOS know we're tailing her."

He clapped Caleb's back, then glanced at his partner. "We better get back—don't need to risk being seen." He glanced over toward Rae. "You sure you can handle Miss Prescott? She doesn't look so hot." He half-grinned. "Sure puts up a good front, though, doesn't she?"

Caleb shoved his hands deep in his pants pockets. "I can take care of Miss Prescott," he stated with a soft emphasis not lost on the other man. One of J.W.'s eyebrows arched, and he loped down the street, shaking his head.

Caleb returned to Rae. She was struggling to re-braid her hair with shaking hands, tears slipping silently down her pale cheeks. Before he could help himself, Caleb gathered her in his arms and hugged her close. Rae stiffened, struggling weakly.

"You don't have to baby me. I'm—" her voice caught, "—I'm okay."

"I'm not babying you." He cupped her face, his thumbs tenderly wiping away the tears. "I'm trying to comfort and reassure you, as any proper guardian angel would under similar circum-stances." He dropped a light kiss on her brow. "You know, if this keeps up, I'm going to petition the Lord for a *real* guardian angel to take up the slack."

"I suppose rescuing me all the time would get pretty wearing." Her voice cracked again, and with an inarticulate little exclamation, she buried her head against his chest. "I'm sorry, Caleb."

He barely heard the muffled words. Holding her close, stroking her hair, her back, he felt a wave of protective compassion so strong it almost knocked the wind out of him. It was not an entirely comfortable emotion, coupled as it was with a cold determination to track down her attackers, and the unpleasant realization that it would be humanly impossible for him to protect Rae twenty-four hours a day, regardless of all his skill, all his training.

CHAPTER 16

"You're a right proper mess." Karen set a mug of tea in front of Rae. "You say he only kissed your palms before he left?"

Rae wrapped her sore hands around the mug and carefully crossed her skinned knee over the unskinned one. Scabs were already forming on all the scraped areas, but between the redness and the Merthiolate Caleb had so liberally applied, she looked like the refugee from a Red Cross demonstration.

It was a sunny morning, with balmy April breezes and a predicted high in the sixties. But the hot mug of tea was exactly what Rae needed. "Karen, do you *ever* think of anything else? Caleb had a job to do, and just because. . .just because. . . ."

"Yes?" Karen drawled, one eyebrow raised and her hand resting knowingly on her hip. "Just because the last six weeks or so he's stuck closer to you than eggs on a hot sidewalk. . .and just because he kisses you every time you purse your lips—even if last night it *was* just your hands. . .you're going to tell me it's all in the line of duty?"

She dropped down across from Rae, propping her chin in her hands. "Honey, ya'll have it bad, and I don't know why you just don't admit it. He might not be the first guy you'd pick out of a crowd, but he's got—" she frowned then shrugged, "—*presence* is the word that comes to mind. Sort of a quiet power, like a sleeping lion."

Rae sipped her tea and avoided meeting Karen's eloquent gaze. "I'd hate to be around when he got awakened," she muttered, thinking of the expression on Caleb's face when he left her the previous night. She sighed, pushed the mug aside and rose. "I better get to the store. It's almost nine."

"Are you going to ignore what you feel, Rae?"

"Karen, right now it's the only way I can keep my sanity. I've

91

been mugged, threatened, almost run down—and the authorities suspect me of everything from conspiracy to fraud to sabotage. If I dwell on what Caleb thinks of me, and what I feel for him, I don't think I'd be able to stay in control."

"Great. Lose control. It'd be good for you."

"See you later, Karen. Thanks for the tea."

"I thought you were supposed to let God be in control, anyway," Karen called after her as she started down the steps of the apartment where Karen lived above the restaurant.

Rae stiffened, hesitated, then kept walking. "He takes care of the big things," she replied, tossing the words over her shoulder. "I'll take care of my life."

She opened the store, her mood subdued. Karen's words bothered her, even rankled a little. Ever since she was a child, she had determined the course of her life so that she would never again feel the yawning helplessness, the frightening uncertainty that had scarred her early years. Accepting Christ as her Savior had given her joy and a measure of peace. Now, Caleb Myers, IOS, and the Starseeker case had erupted into her life.

She checked all the music, dusted the shelves and her treasures, and tried to pretend everything was normal. When the bell tinkled an hour later, she looked up from the counter in relief. "Good morning. May I help you?"

A young woman smiled brightly and bounced over to the counter. The sleeves of her oversized shirt flapped as her arms gestured around the rooms. "This is the most awesome store! I heard about it from a friend." Propping her elbows on the countertop, she confided with engaging candor. "Everyone at church keeps begging me to do a mini-concert, and my friend Elaine promised me you have the best selection of Christian music in the Springs. So—" she waved her arm again, "I need at least half a dozen songs. I've got some, but I'd like to try some new stuff. Can you help me? Say, what happened to your hands?"

"I scraped them." Rae came round the counter and headed

for the appropriate room. "All the music you'll need will be in here. Why don't you tell me some of the songs you've done, and we'll take it from there?"

A pleasant half hour went by, with a satisfactory pile of sheet music accumulating. Rae found her customer's attention strayed occasionally, her eyes darting around the store as she asked questions. How long had Rae lived there? What was her training? Why didn't she want to move?

Eventually the inquisitive, talkative young woman decided she had enough, and Rae gathered up the pieces. After tallying the total, she waited while the girl rummaged in her purse for the money.

"That's a lovely necklace you're wearing," Rae commented. Her forehead wrinkled in a frown. "It's very unusual, but for some reason it looks familiar. Are you sure you've never been in here before?"

The girl's hand flew up to the necklace, almost as if she were trying to hide it. "No," she answered with a bright, brittle laugh. "I'm sure you'd remember me, anyway, wouldn't you? How many customers buy as much music as I have?"

Rae took the proffered bills and busied herself at the cash register. "Actually, I'm not too good with faces," she confessed, "but your necklace is so unusual. . . ."

"I have to be going. Thanks for your help." The girl scooped up the music, accepted her change, and walked out swiftly.

Rae shook her head. *I hope I didn't offend her. I wonder how I can learn to remember people better?* Even Det. Grabowski had not been able to hide his frustration and impatience with her lack of observation skills.

She paused, examining her scraped hands. On the other hand, maybe her lack of awareness was the only reason she was nursing a few scrapes instead of lying in the morgue.

How long was it going to last? With a toss of her head, Rae picked up the phone to call Karen and share the wonderful news of her forty-seven dollar sale. She'd also call Jerry at church and chat with him awhile; if nothing else, she could try to bore IOS to death listening to her decidedly non-intriguing conversations.

Caleb pulled up in front of the FBI field office in Colorado Springs, where he had arranged to meet with Tray Ramirez. He was restless today, his internal radar sending out disquieting warning signals.

Five minutes later he found out why.

"It's not looking so hot for Miss Prescott," Tray informed him bluntly. He indicated a report on his desk, and Caleb picked it up, memorizing the contents while Tray talked. "As you see, Fisher's had two deposits of fifteen thousand dollars in the past two months—and the same amount has been withdrawn from Miss Prescott's savings account."

"She has no knowledge of that account, Tray. I'll ask her about it when I see her later, but I'm not going to push. I have a feeling you've done enough of that lately."

"I understand how you feel, Myers, but the account *is* in her name." The phone buzzed, and he snatched it up, spoke briefly, then hung up. He studied Caleb thoughtfully a moment. "Let's discuss Fisher since Rae Prescott is such a touchy issue."

Caleb dropped into a chair. "What in particular?" He tugged on the lock of hair falling over his forehead, his mind's eye still seeing the condemning set of figures in the report. *Rae*, he thought, *what kind of trap has been laid for you?*

"You're more familiar with computers and computer types," Tray countered. "Why would Fisher jeopardize his career to get involved with IOS? His record's clean, and his personal life sounds positively dull. Married right out of college, divorced three years later. No discernible relationships since. Friends and colleagues think he's your average, quiet, retiring type guy. So why get caught up with a bunch of traitors?"

Caleb finally left his hair alone, relaxing back in the chair and stretching out his legs. "Any number of reasons," he drawled sadly. "In Fisher's case, my guess is that it goes beyond money, although that probably figures in it as well."

"Doesn't it always?"

"It's almost a cliche any more, isn't it?" Caleb agreed. He exchanged world-weary looks with the FBI agent. "Anyway— you've seen Fisher. Unassuming, balding, slight. The antithesis of the popular Hollywood hunk. I read an article a year or so ago on computer viruses and their perpe-trators. The author theorized about a pattern of personalities he dubbed the 'nerd syndrome.' Fisher's history fits that. He had very few friends all through school, spent all his spare time with computers."

Tray leaned back, hands over his head. "I got labeled as a Latino troublemaker when I was in high school." He looked across at Caleb. "But I didn't turn into a statistic—or a criminal. Fisher might've gotten dumped on—and I'm sorry. But even a so-called 'nerd' can overcome the label."

"People have different breaking points," Caleb murmured. "Devising a virus program could have started out as a simple prank and deteriorated to the sabotage. I've cross-checked all Fisher's records, though, and like you say, there's no history of aberrant or malicious behavior." He paused, then finished quietly, "We'll just have to keep digging. I'm convinced Fisher is involved, but not that he's the head guy."

"What about Ray Prescott, Rae's father?" He shook his head. "Can you imagine naming your daughter after you—then skipping out on her?" Riffling through some more files, he tugged one out and scanned it briefly. "He's definitely a loser, but the profile doesn't fit an IOS exec."

"Neither does his daughter."

There was a short, tense silence, Then Ramirez threw up his hands. "I *know* she's the stereotypical picture of innocence. I *know* she's gone out of her way to cooperate with us." He leveled a piercing look at Caleb. "And I know your emotions have gotten involved. The only reason I haven't demanded that you be thrown off the case is the strength of your reputation."

"Thanks." Caleb's voice was unruffled. "Then you'll bear that in mind when I continue to reject her involvement with IOS. How long since the Denver guys checked on the signature or signatures which can authorize the withdrawal of deposits from Rae's account?"

"They should get back to me by this afternoon. Dennis Hoffman's our liaison. He's supposed to contact me."

"I'd appreciate the update. I'm going to Falcon to talk with Archie Cohen again. They're still trying to track the virus and how it made it to the mainframe. I promised to see what I could do. If I'm not at Joyful Noise or my motel room later, just leave a message with the agents staking out the store."

He rose and headed for the door.

"What makes you so sure the Prescott woman is innocent?" Tray called after him.

His voice was conciliatory, genuinely curious. Caleb turned. "Because I can see all the way into her soul when I look in her eyes," he replied. "She doesn't have the right kind of defenses, Tray. She hasn't needed any with the kind of life she leads."

"Just because she's religious and runs a music store doesn't make her incapable of deceit."

"I'd agree with you if Rae was religious," Caleb said very softly. "But she's not. She's a Christian." His gaze bore into the abruptly confused eyes of the agent. "Think about it, Tray. And while you're at it, think about this: if any of your guys relax their guard, and Rae suffers because of it—I'll be on your back faster than a bolt of chain lightning in the clouds."

He closed the door with ominous gentleness.

CHAPTER 17

Rae was sipping tea and reading a how-to book on basic self-defense when Caleb arrived. She waited until he rang the bell and knocked in the distinctive pattern they had devised, then scurried down the short hall to let him in.

"A month ago I would have felt silly taking these elaborate precautions," she confessed nervously as they walked back to the kitchen. *Did he know about the savings account?*

She busied herself by fixing him a glass of lemonade.

"I know." Caleb came up behind her, and his hand brushed lightly over her cheek. "How are you doing? Did all your students and customers make a fuss over your battle wounds?"

Rae rolled her eyes, her smile barely forced. "I had two students who insisted I should be in bed—probably because neither one of them had practiced."

She knew her voice was far too bright and artificial, and she tried to soften the frantic tone creeping in through the words. "Most of the customers were either too polite to say anything—or they didn't care. Now my friend Karen, on the other hand. . . ."

"I don't think I want to hear what Karen had to say," Caleb allowed. "She probably thinks we ought to call out the National Guard and have them trail you in perfect formation."

"That about sums it up." *Except for her pointed remarks about our relationship*, Rae added to herself. There was no way she would bring *that* up, however.

"What is this?" He had moved over to the trestle table and picked up the book she had been reading. Shaking his head, he flipped through the pages, put the book down, and turned to Rae. "It's impossible to learn adequate self-defense from a book."

"I'm quite aware of that," Rae returned with a bite to the words. *Was he going to mention that account?* "But it was better than just sitting around feeling like a sitting duck all the time." She paused. "Have you found out anything new, Caleb? That you can share with me?"

He patted the bench beside him, but Rae slid in across from him, her hands tensing at the abruptly shuttered look that blanked all the indulgent warmth from his face. "You know something, don't you? Is it about my father? Or—or something else?"

He studied her, propping his elbows on the table and resting his chin on the palm of his hand. "Rae, will you tell me about your childhood? What do you remember about your parents— besides a memory of long hair and fringes? Every time the subject comes up, you shut down like a computer given the 'Escape' command."

Rae focused on Caleb's fingers, mentally reciting Scripture to achieve the necessary calm. "I don't discuss my past because I feel it's irrelevent to the person I am now. It's also very painful, as I've told you before."

"The last thing I want to do," Caleb said, "is to cause you more pain. But, Rae. . .your father *is* involved with IOS. And regardless of whether or not your own involvement in the Starseeker case is incidental or planned, you have nonetheless become pivotal to the investigation."

Scripture verses and serenity scattered like startled pigeons. Hot color stormed her cheeks. "I am not a criminal!" she sputtered, almost incoherent. "Just because my father is, doesn't make me one, too."

She stood up, hurt and angry because, of all people, she thought Caleb would understand. "It's that stupid account, isn't it? Agent Ramirez told you about that account, and now you think. . .you think. . . ."

Squeezing her eyes and her mouth shut, Rae tried to stiffen her shoulders against the onslaught of pain. She should have known. She had learned by the time she was four years old that men were an undependable lot of self-serving egotists.

Except for Uncle Floyd. And even if he had lavished her with love and material possessions, she hadn't been able to depend on him or her brother. Love, riddled with guilt and compensation, had sent Frank to the other side of the country, drowning his past in the pursuit of money.

And Rae had given up in an illustrious career to hold onto an antiquated legacy she could neither deny or relinquish.

Caleb stood up, too, and moved to her side, putting his hands on her shoulders. "You misunderstood me," he started to say, but Rae pulled free.

"All these weeks, leading me on, treating me like—like I was someone special." She raked him head to foot with a blistering, condemnatory glare. "I'm surprised you haven't had me put behind bars already, seeing what a dangerous felon I am."

Caleb stuffed his hands in the back pockets of his wheat-colored jeans and directed his gaze to the ceiling. "Actually, I think your temper is more dangerous than your nefarious tendencies," he mused. "Especially when you jump to such ridiculous conclusions."

His eyes burned a molten gold path into her soul. "I believe you when you say you don't know anything about that savings account, Rae."

Suddenly she was in his arms, tugged into a close embrace with such lazy speed she was too bewildered to struggle. One of his hands wrapped around the loose braid spilling down her back, tugging her head so she was forced to meet head-on the glowing fire in his eyes.

She had a feeling her wayward tongue had just flicked the sleeping lion one too many times.

"I believe in your innocence totally, little cat's claw," he breathed, his mouth hovering just above hers. "And I'm spending every hour I'm not with you trying to establish it beyond doubt to everyone else."

"Caleb—"

"But you're going to have to trust me." He dropped a light, teasing kiss on her half-parted lips. "Trust me both as a man—and as a Christian. If I can see Christ's love shining out of your eyes, won't you try to see the same thing in mine?"

Rae swallowed, dizzy with all the sensations bombarding her senses. "I can't see anything when you hold me like this," she muttered breathlessly, her eyes drifting shut because she was burning up in the flames of his. Her hands slowly relaxed, resting against his chest instead of pushing. "You don't play fair, Mr. Myers."

A chuckle floated past her ear. "How so, Miss Prescott?" His hand released her braid to cup her cheek, the fingers pressing with restrained tenderness.

Rae opened her eyes, took a shallow catch-breath. "I've never known a man like you." Her own fingers, graceful only at the piano, lifted hesitantly to touch his hard cheekbone. "Do you really believe in me, Caleb?"

She watched the tiny laugh lines at the corners of his eyes deepen. "So much that I put my career on the line over it," he admitted cheerfully. His thumb rubbed a caressing circle, and Rae felt the blossoming heat radiate from her flushed cheeks all the way down to her toes.

"Why?" she asked, unable to fathom the risk he was taking in her behalf. Shaking her head slowly, she repeated the question. "Why?"

The teasing laughter faded as he studied her upturned face with a solemn intensity that would have been intimidating in another man. "I've asked myself that question a lot lately." With almost absentminded gentleness he began stroking fallen wisps of hair from her face. "There's something about you—I feel you pushing me away with one hand—but reaching out with the other. I see the evidence of your faith in the way you live, in your inner strength—yet I sense a fear, almost as if you're afraid to really trust God to take care of you. To let Him control your life completely—in every area."

Caleb dropped his hands, sat back down and took a long drink of lemonade, then stared down into the glass as if memorizing the position of the ice cubes. "I don't like the way you make me feel—but every time I try to ignore it, or push it aside, it just comes back stronger." He flicked Rae a brief, lancing look as potent as a touch. "It's almost as if God keeps using the circumstances to throw us together, forcing me to face what I'm feeling."

Rae flopped back down across from him, gestured awkwardly with her hand. "Caleb, I—" she started to say, but her hand knocked over her mug of tea. Muttering largely incoherent streams of self-abuse and disgust, she mopped up the mess, then dumped the mug in the sink. By the time she returned to the table, the stingingly personal moment had passed.

"I'm feeling pretty mixed-up myself," she agreed with careful neutrality. "If you're the only one who thinks I'm not part of the conspiracy, is the reason for the set-up across the street for my protection—or to try and catch me passing government secrets?" She hesitated, then added defiantly, "Probably to my father, who plans to sell them to any foreign government willing to pay the highest price for the technology."

"I think we're back to square one," Caleb murmured. He drank the rest of the lemonade, then set the glass down with elaborate care. "Rae, half the reason everyone is so suspicious of you is because of your adamant refusal to talk about your past."

"I'm sure the savings account of which I knew nothing figures pretty prominently."

Caleb sighed and steepled his fingers. "That, too—now," he assented wearily. "Not to mention the fact that our chief suspect has had two large deposits made in the last two months—with matching withdrawals from your account."

"What?" Rae gasped, feeling a snake pit yawning at her feet. "Caleb. . ." her voice hoarsened. "I have no idea of how that account was established. I don't!"

"I know. I know. But can you see how I'm scrabbling for leads? Any details you could remember about your father could help. A name, a place—anything. Help me prove your innocence, Rae."

"I thought I *was* innocent until proven guilty." Her fingers played jerkily over the woodgrained tabletop. "I wonder if this was how Jesus felt. Everyone kept trying to frame Him, too."

"He also promised the truth would set you free. Help us find that truth—even if it's painful. Yes, IOS is framing you—but I don't want it to lead to something worse."

Rae glanced across at his grim face, feeling the bitterness, the helplessness well up and spill between them. "Maybe when IOS succeeds, all your cronies will finally believe I *was* just an innocent pawn. Maybe I should draw up a list of the songs I'd like played for my funeral."

Caleb slouched back in the seat, his body the epitome of relaxation. "Don't be so melodramatic," he chastised her with a careful lack of emphasis that nonetheless stung. "You—and Joyful Noise—are being watched for both reasons, yes. We're pretty certain the store *is* being used as a drop; when we figure out how, we ought to be able to pin some concrete evidence on the parties involved—and you'll be safe."

"But in the meantime I just sit around waiting for the next abduction, or a fire bomb to be tossed through the window." She flounced up, her temper flaring anew because Caleb just sat there as laid back as a cat in sunshine. "I don't like this, Caleb. I feel horrible—helpless, exposed."

"I know. We're working round the clock on it."

"Then why is it taking so long?"

He snagged one of her flailing arms and unhurriedly forced her to sit down beside him. "Because, while we have a suspect, and a lot of hypotheses—we haven't established motive, method, or the others involved. All that takes time. Months, probably."

His arm came round her shoulders and hugged her to him. Rae was unable to resist the craven need to sink into the calm and comfort he offered. "I know," she admitted in a sheepish little voice. "It's just that I feel like such a coward for being so afraid—and that makes me angry with myself for not claiming all the promises that God will take care of us." She bit her lip. "I detest feeling so out of control, so helpless to do anything concrete."

"I know the feeling," Caleb returned. "I know the feeling very well."

Rae swiveled her head upward, wondering at the nuance of haunting fear that underlay the words.

Caleb feathered a kiss across her forehead. "When I ran across the street yesterday and hurled us both in the gutter, I came as close to panic as I have in all the years I've been an agent." His mouth brushed tenderly against the straggling wisps of hair at her temple. "Maybe I should've specialized in terrorism instead of computer sabotage."

The arm holding her close tightened. "I've had to face the fact that I can't be here twenty-four hours a day to watch over you, to keep you safe."

He paused, then added softly, "I guess we both better start leaning a little more on some of God's promises, hadn't we?"

CHAPTER 18

Rae's mail the next afternoon included a handwritten note from Caleb. "I didn't have time to come by, and you know I couldn't call. I have a lead on your father, and am flying to California to follow up on it. Be careful, little cat's claw—and keep your chin up. P.S. Read Psalm 32:7. Caleb."

Rae's first reaction was gratefulness that this time, at least, he had let her know where he was going. But as the afternoon wore on, her grateful mood eroded into one of disgruntlement, then unrighteous indignation. She decided that the tone of the note, instead of being reassuring, smacked of patronization—almost as if she were a whining little girl who needed pacifying.

And that ridiculous nickname. He had called her that a couple of other times, and she had finally commented in an ultra-polite voice that she didn't really appreciate the comparison.

With that melting grin that poured over her like warm honey on a biscuit, Caleb explained that he was referring to a species of wildflower. "Beautiful blooms, but loads of tiny little curved thorns just waiting to scratch the unwary."

He had stopped her indignant rebuttal with a swift kiss. "You're a sensitive, beautiful, caring woman, Rae—but that temper of yours can draw blood. You can also be more stubborn than any of my three sisters ever thought about being. . . ."

Rae re-read the note for the umpteenth time, her memory transforming the harmless explanation into a flame which ignited her combustible temper. If Caleb Myers thought he could disappear with no more explanation than a flimsy little note that told her absolutely nothing, he *better* armor himself against her claws.

"You have a lead on *my* father—and you expect me to just sit here and pretend life is normal," she muttered beneath her breath as she furiously tallied the day's receipts. "Normal—ha! For almost two months now I've—"

The bell jangled and the nervous little man who collected old sheet music scuttled crab-like over to the desk. Rae tried to smooth her temper. "Hello." She forced a smile.

His mouth twitched upward briefly. "I know it's late, but I was wondering if you'd let me rummage a few minutes." He glanced at his watch. "You close at five-thirty? That gives me about ten minutes."

"Well—were you looking for anything in particular?" She tried to be compliant, but her mood was too volatile. Mr. Fowler—no, Fisher, she thought he'd told her—happened to be looking at Caleb's note, left lying beside the ledger.

Rae followed his glance. Before she could control it, her hand snatched the note up, crumpling it. "Go ahead and look around," she all but snapped. "I'll finish some work here."

"Thanks." He looked from her clenched hand holding the wadded paper to her temper-heated face. "Problems?" he probed hesitantly.

"No—no. I'm just, uh, out of sorts." She waved an irritable hand toward the classical room. "You better rummage if you're going to."

She tried to concentrate on the ledger, but between Caleb's note and an intruding awareness that Mr. Fisher kept darting her questioning, concerned glances, Rae made three mistakes in as many minutes. She threw the pencil down, picked up the offending note, and with sudden fury ripped it into tiny pieces.

"Why are you tearing it up? What on earth made you so upset?"

Rae's head snapped with a jerk. Mr. Fisher had come back to the desk, and was eyeing her with the bug-eyed concern of a fly about to become the frog's dinner.

"It's just a note that made me mad—and I really don't see why you should be so interested." She swept the miniscule scraps into her palm and dropped them with a flourish in the wastebasket. "Did you find any music you wanted?"

His gaze whipped from the trash to her face, then his head jerked toward the classical music room. "Not today," he replied, his voice as a sharp and wary as Rae's.

She suddenly realized her behavior bordered on the inexcusable, especially toward a customer. Biting her lip, she tried to smile. "I'm sorry, Mr. Fisher," she offered, her voice contrite. "I shouldn't have snapped at you."

"That's okay." He backed away, his glance moving almost furtively around the store.

Rae frowned. "Mr. Fisher? I really am sorry. Listen—I'm expecting a shipment of music from a store that went out of business in Aurora. . . ."

"Um, yes. I'll be back." He wiped his forehead, then scuttled back out, his hunched-over shoulders and shuffling gait more crab-like than ever.

I really did it that time, Rae scolded herself ruefully. Caleb was right. Her temper did inflict wounds, and for a Christian who knew better, she deserved whatever rebuke the Lord meted out. *I've just got to control it better,* she decided, shaking her head and bending over the ledger.

Restless and keyed up, Rae decided to run errands after supper. She carefully bolted and locked the back door, resisting the urge to wave at whomever was on duty on the upper level of her garage. The novelty had worn thin. The cutting edge of terror might have dulled, but the oppressive awareness that she was always watched taxed her already painfully stretched nerves. Her skin crawled every time she left the house, prickling with the uncomfortable sensation of a cold axe blade pressing against her neck.

She turned the car radio on to the Christian station she listened to, and reminded herself that God always had His eye trained upon her, too. With sudden resolution, she changed lanes, then turned and headed for church.

Using the key she had been given, she unlocked one of the

106

doors, then hurried to the alarm system. All she needed was a squad car roaring up here to arrest her as a burglar.

After unlocking the sound room, she flicked on just enough light to allow her to see the synthesizer and the grand piano. Selecting the music for Sunday's worship service, she spent a couple of pleasant hours playing, trying different blends, layering and re-layering until she found combinations she liked. Then she moved to the piano, where she practiced another hour.

By nine she was tired, and the last dregs of guilt and tension from her outburst with Mr. Fisher had dwindled away. Refreshed, determined to control her temper with the same discipline she exerted on her music, she turned off all the lights, reset the alarm, and opened the door to leave.

Two men stepped forward out of the shadows as it closed behind her.

"Miss Prescott?"

Rae gasped and half-screamed before it occurred to her that they might be the men assigned to follow her. "You nearly scared me to death!" she began, and stopped. "Who are you?" What if—she clutched the key in her hand and surreptitiously gauged the distance to the door lock.

There was a split-second pause before the taller of the two men answered. "Getting a little more careful, are we, Miss Prescott?" His hand moved suddenly, lifting a flashlight and shining it directly in Rae's face. "All the bruises are gone. How would you feel about acquiring some new ones?"

The other man, short and stocky and as wide as a bulldozer, crowded Rae away from the door and toward a dark corner the outside lighting failed to reach. A nauseating odor of sweat, cigar smoke, and peppermint swirled up Rae's flaring nostrils.

"What do you want?" she demanded with a show of bravado, trying to shield her eyes from the flashlight.

The tall man laughed softly, and the sound raised the hair on the back of Rae's neck. He turned off the flashlight, then casually reached out and enclosed her throat. Large, abnormally smooth fingers pressed lightly, warningly. "You've made some people very nervous, Miss Prescott. Just as nervous as me and my associate here are making you." The fingers pressed a little harder, and Rae flinched.

"You *are* nervous, aren't you, Miss Prescott?" he murmured in a sibilant, chilling whisper.

"I'm petrified and you know it!" Rae gasped out, wondering where the plainclothesmen who were supposed to tail her were. She wanted to throw the knowledge in these two creeps' faces, but she couldn't. She refused to break anyone's cover, regardless of her personal safety. *Father, does that make me incredibly brave—or incredibly stupid?*

She tried to swallow. "What do you want?" she asked again, the words emerging as more of a thin croak.

An eerie chuckle grated against the roaring in her ears. "This is a second—friendly—warning, Miss Prescott. Regardless of what you notice or are told—you keep your mouth shut. And if you happen onto any—shall we say, information—then. . . ."

The hand squeezed again, and Rae's hands reached up to claw. She might as well have tried to claw an iron pipe.

"Then," the voice hissed, "you better not destroy that information."

She was freed, and sucked gulps of air into her depleted lungs. Two hands on her shoulders squeezed from behind, and a gust of peppermint-laden breath threatened to choke off the fresh air. "You also better warn your boyfriend to keep his nose out of your business."

Peppermint-breath's voice was rough, less polished than the taller man's. Rae backed into the brick wall, feeling the cold roughness scrape her elbows and shoulderblades.

"He might enjoy playing hero, but the next time he comes to the rescue might be his last."

Their bulky silhouettes faded into the night with a noise-lessness more terrifying than the thundering of a herd of enraged elephants.

CHAPTER 19

Fingers shaking so badly she was barely able to fit the key in the lock to activate the alarm, Rae briefly debated deliberately setting it off. Where were her two shadows, as she had dubbed the agents assigned to watch her at all times?

She crept, step by fearful step, toward her car which sat blissfully alone under the parking lot security lights. Collapsing behind the steering wheel, she waited for her ears to stop ringing, her heartbeat to settle, and tried to think.

Ever since she had almost been sideswiped, she had been kept on a short leash. The men who monitored her every move might be invisible to the innocent bystander, but Rae couldn't even dash to the 7-Eleven without a discreet escort.

If they hadn't charged to the rescue tonight, it was probably because they figured she wasn't in mortal danger, so they chose not to compromise their cover. The Starseeker case obviously took precedence over a mere individual whose innocence was still questionable.

Indignation restored enough courage for Rae to drive home. She had just turned off Academy Boulevard when a flashing red light illuminated her rearview mirror. She pulled into a parking lot and stopped.

"What's wrong, officer?" Rae only rolled the window down a few inches. "There isn't a sign preventing a right turn on red at this intersection, and I know I wasn't speeding."

The patrolman grinned reassuringly. "I'm just delivering a message, Miss Prescott. If you'll turn into that hamburger place and order yourself a milkshake, someone will happen along who wants to talk to you."

"I'll just bet they do!" Rae shot back. She thanked the police officer, nodded her head, and watched him discreetly follow until she was in the parking lot.

The only customers in the restaurant left as Rae sat down in a booth all the way in the back. She took a sip of the unwanted milkshake and waited.

A few minutes later a short, compactly built man in jeans and CSU T-shirt strolled down the aisle. Rae recognized the man as the detective who had run over after Caleb rescued her from being sideswiped.

"Well, hello, Rae! Long time, no see." He slid into the booth across from her. Without seeming to, his eye roved over the restaurant, and he relaxed infinitesimally. Taking a huge bite out of a chicken sandwich, he turned his shrewd gaze on Rae, studying her while he chewed. "Are you okay?" he asked quietly.

"Where were you?" Rae attacked, smarting anew at the thought that he and his partner had witnessed the whole humiliating scene.

"Close enough to help if you really needed it," the detective promised. He leaned forward. "Listen, Miss Prescott—Rae—it's fairly obvious that right now they don't want to kill you. They're still too uncertain of your part in all of it. Now—can you tell me what they said? Try to remember exactly, so Ramirez and Grabowski won't override Myers and have you wired."

Rae shuddered at the thought. She dutifully recounted the frightening episode, faintly apologetic when it was obvious she had provided nothing tangible for the authorities to use.

"Seems like my only part in this whole mess is to provide local IOS heavies with a punching bag." She stirred the thick shake with short, almost vicious swirls. "I realize you want to catch whoever sabotaged that tracking program out at Falcon, but I wish you guys—and the IOS thugs—would accept the fact that I don't know *anything*!"

The detective leaned back. His light gray eyes dissected her with cool detachment. "As long as IOS thinks you might constitute a threat, or be hatching some sort of double-cross, the feds can't afford to treat you merely as a dupe."

His gaze narrowed when fresh exasperation flooded Rae's cheeks. "Especially when there's that account in Denver. And your father."

"I told you—"

He lifted a placating hand. "I know. And Myers insists you're as pure as the first snowfall on Pikes Peak."

"Thanks a bunch," Rae muttered. She glared across the table. "What's your name, anyway? Or is that another piece of information I don't need to know?"

"J.W. Ayer," he returned equably. Suddenly he smiled. "You've got guts, Rae Prescott. I'll have to give you credit. Most women would have thrown a screaming fit back there at your church. Evan and I halfway expected you to yell for us, knowing we'd be somewhere close."

"I didn't want to blow your cover."

"Thanks. We do appreciate that—and I know you were scared." He paused, adding more gently, "That's why I took a chance and arranged this meeting."

He finished his sandwich, and Rae's throat muscles relaxed enough for her to sip the shake. "Can you tell me if you've found out anything about the man responsible for planting the virus program?" she asked.

J.W.'s head lifted sharply. "How do you know it's a man?" he shot at her. "And who told you about the virus? Myers?" He muttered something beneath his breath Rae pretended not to hear.

"I assumed it was a man." She shoved the rest of the milkshake aside. "And since I'm involved in this whether I invited it or not, Caleb thought it advisable to tell me a little bit about the case." She glared at J.W. "I've spent some time reading up on virus programs, and I'm cooperating as much as I can with the FBI, not to mention you and your boss. Don't treat me like an imbecil—I'm not."

"I'm aware of that." One light brown eyebrow lifted. "You

111

play the piano like a dream—I understand you were planning to go professional until your uncle died."

Rae nodded. "I suppose I could have eventually made enough money to justify what he provided for my training—but I couldn't afford to let the house sit empty."

The detective nodded. He half-smiled a little sheepishly. "There's a piece you play a lot at night, when Evan and I have to pull the graveyard shift. We can hear over the mini-bugs you let the FBI plant in your living quarters. What's it called?"

Disconcerted, she stared at him. "Can you hum a little of it?"

Red stained the bridge of his nose and cheeks. "I've got a voice like a cement mixer," he confessed. "It goes all over the keyboard—sounds like you have about six hands."

"Mm. . .probably 'The Lord is my Light'." She shoved the emptied containers aside and played the opening bars on the table, singing the words softly but clearly. "Like that?"

"That's it—it's a religious song, then?"

"I think of it as a Christian song, and it's one of my favorites, too." She watched her fingers playing the table a second longer, then quit. "I guess I've been playing it a lot lately because the words really help me right now. They remind me that I don't need to be afraid of anything, because God is taking care of me."

J.W. shifted. "I never put much stock in that stuff," he offered gruffly. "But I suppose if it helps you cope, I'm all for it."

"That *stuff* kept me from having a screaming fit at the church earlier, not to mention giving me the courage—or stupidity—to keep from calling you for help," she said calmly, then grinned. "And that song's been on my mind over a month now, ever since this woman wanted a copy. She's been in a couple of times, and I never seem to remember her, except she wore this necklace. . . ." Rae shook her head. "I'm rambling—sorry."

"What kind of necklace?"

Rae shrugged. "I'd never seen one like it—until another

112

customer came in wearing what I'm sure was exactly the same thing. I probably put my foot in it—I haven't seen either one in awhile now."

J.W. leaned forward. "Describe the necklaces."

His voice was level, but an undercurrent of excitement, almost urgency, rippled beneath the quiet words. Rae bit her lip. "It was silver and turquoise," she replied slowly, "but there was also some pearl-like stone as well. And while Old Colorado has similar jewelry on practically every corner, I'd never seen this particular design."

She glanced across the table. "It was unusual enough that even I remembered it. There was a large thunderbird at the bottom, with two small ones interspersed with whatever that other stone is on either side." She spread her hands helplessly. "I'm sorry. That's sort of a garbled description, and Det. Grabowski grumbles about my lamentable observation skill every time I see him. But—"

"You've done great." J.W. was beaming at her, looking so pleased and excited that Rae's jaw dropped. His hand reached across and patted hers. "This just might be the break we're looking for."

At Rae's look of utter mystification, he relented. "Ramirez told us that occasionally IOS females use that method to identify themselves."

"A thunderbird necklace?"

"Not necessarily *that* necklace—I'm referring to the use of jewelry. According to Ramirez, there have been two other recorded cases where jewelry was used as the ID code."

Rae, mentally trying to summon up a description of the two women, did not notice how closely Det. Ayer was watching her.

"Can you describe the women wearing the necklaces?" he asked in an eerie echo of her turbulent thoughts.

"That's what I was trying to do. I knew you'd be asking." She shook her head helplessly. "One was probably in her late

113

thirties—and she didn't know much about music. The other one was young—she bought a whole pile of music. Christian, mostly solos she said she planned to sing."

"Hair? Eye color? Weight? Distinguishing marks?"

Rae ducked her head in embarrassment and chagrin. "I can tell you the music they bought," she offered. "Title, publisher, date of publication, and how much it cost. But as far as anything else. . . ."

J.W. grimaced. "Well, it won't do much good if you don't at least *try* to remember what Grabowski told you. You're supposed to keep a record of anything out of the ordinary." He gathered the trash, stood. "Why didn't you mention the necklaces before?"

She finally noticed the undercurrent of suspicion. "It just didn't occur to me," she replied, weariness making the words drag. "I suppose you're thinking it was deliberate, aren't you?"

"One of the things you learn when you've been on the street as long as I have," the detective returned just as wearily, "is that the most angelic face can hide a devil's soul."

He looked down at Rae. "Myers is a solid guy, for a fed. I hope he's right about those guileless eyes of yours, and all that talk about your Christian faith is more than a bunch of words."

He nodded once, then sauntered out the door with the wily grace of an alley cat.

CHAPTER 20

The L.A. precinct office in which Caleb sat offered a relatively calm oasis compared to the chaos and noise outside the semi-private, glassed-in walls. Drunks, dope-peddlers, prostitutes, criminals and their victims. . .society's dregs milled around, waiting with apathy, defiance, or hope for the system to take its grinding course.

Det. Harold Zeingold sipped a lukewarm cup of coffee and ran gnarled, ink-stained fingers through the thinning wisps of his salt and pepper hair. Deep lines scored his forehead, running down his nose to his mouth. It was the stubborn, cynical face of a man who had seen and heard everything.

"Sorry I can't do more for you," he offered in a rumbly bass voice that sounded more matter-of-fact than apologetic. "But if the statement we got before he was blown away helps, I'm glad. T-bone was one of our more reliable snitches." He shook his head and watched Caleb reading the single page document.

"I'll need a copy of this."

Zeingold waved his hand. "Sure. Keep me posted. Prescott's a sneaky, two-bit hustler, but he's gotten himself some good connections. Since they're IOS connections, you guys have your work cut out for you."

"I know," Caleb assented. He twisted his watchband. "I'm pretty sure he'll surface in Denver within the next couple of weeks. This—" he held up the statement from the dead informant, "—pretty much insures that. I'm concerned about his daughter, though. I'm convinced Prescott is using her."

Zeingold grunted. "Are you still also convinced the source leads back down here?"

"Fisher doesn't have the personality to spearhead an operation this size. He could be the brains behind formatting and

115

planting the virus, but I think IOS is calling the shots."

He sat forward. "They wouldn't place any of their top people that close to their victim, especially when it's the U.S. government and a top secret project. It's too risky. Southern California has the anonymity as well as the potential for milking big bucks to make it rate pretty high on a list of likely headquarters."

Both men shifted their gazes to the opposite wall. Above rows of filing cabinets, the wall was peppered with maps.

"Of course," Caleb continued with a rueful grin, "it could just as easily be D.C. or Denver, Chicago or Miami. They might not even *have* a so-called corporate headquarters."

"Neither," Zeingold reminded him dryly, "does organized crime. I don't envy you the task of trying to run IOS to earth, much less getting a conviction not based on endangerment or entrapment."

"We'll get as many of them as we can," Caleb promised grimly. "DOD gets pretty hostile when someone messes around with multi-million dollar leading edge space technology.

"We're pretty sure," he told Zeingold slowly, "that there's someone in the area instructing Fisher, keeping him in line. And they've sent strong-arm thugs to harass and intimidate Rae Prescott. Any results yet on the descriptions I gave you?"

"Nope. But I doubt if they'd import dirt-bags from this far. Have you checked Denver?"

"I'm flying there this evening."

The door opened and the booking officer poked his head in. "There's a guy out here screaming brutality against Loomis, Lieutenant."

"Who is it?"

"Vinnie. Loomis caught him dealing to a couple of kids."

"Umph," Lt. Zeingold grimaced and hoisted his bulky, six-foot-four body out of the chair. "Knowing Loomis, he might have done more than read him his rights." He paused, adding dryly, "Knowing Vinnie, he probably deserved whatever he got." He glanced at Caleb. "I'll be there in a minute."

Caleb stood as well. "Will you let me know if you hear

116

anything else on IOS? No matter how flimsy or unsubstantiated? The information T-bone provided has been invaluable. I just wish it hadn't been at the cost of his life."

Zeingold shrugged. Caleb knew that to the people-hardened detective, T-bone was nothing more than a useful source of information, not worth crying over.

"I better get moving so I don't miss my flight. The sooner I get to Denver, the sooner I can get back to the Springs, and we can collate all this information."

Zeingold's rugged face split in a wide grin. "You feeling the heat, Myers?"

"We've tried to keep it under wraps. Of course, if we don't get some kind of break soon, I have a feeling Congress is going to be screaming for some heads on a platter." He stuffed his hands in the hip pockets of his jeans. "Probably mine."

Dennis Hoffman, one of the FBI guys out of Denver, met him at Stapleton Airport. It was eleven at night and pouring rain. Hoffman grumbled about the abysmal weather as he drove through the surprisingly heavy traffic on the way to the local Bureau offices.

In a conference room littered with paper coffee cups and crumpled cellophane wrappers, they joined the Denver section chief, Bob Taylor. He gestured Caleb to a chair, then slid a file across the table.

"Rae Prescott's brother is responsible for the savings account," he announced as Caleb sank into the chair. "We got in touch with him this morning. He never told her about the account because he wanted it to be a cushion if the store bombed."

"They aren't that close," Hoffman put in. "From what we've learned, Frank Prescott thinks his sister is too sentimental and idealistic. But he's got enough family feeling to make sure she doesn't end up on welfare."

Caleb rubbed the back of his hand over his mouth and gritty eyes. He had been seventeen hours without sleep, and the flight from L.A. had been bumpy and exhausting. Taylor's stunning revelation poured over his weary bones like the balm of Gilead.

"Thank God," he murmured beneath his breath with heartfelt sincerity. Rapidly scanning the file, his mouth relaxed into a relieved grin. "You're positive the signature on the checks withdrawing the thirty thousand is forged?"

"Yes." Taylor leaned back, absently cracking his knuckles. "It was a good job—and it's the expert opinion of our document examiner that the original sample was done by a man, which pretty much absolves Miss Prescott."

"Maybe you can sleep tonight, Myers," Dennis Hoffman jibed good-naturedly. "Your girlfriend's off the hook."

Caleb was not in the mood for needling, good-natured or not. He shifted slightly, leveling a gelid stare at the agent. After a quiet moment of increasing tension, Hoffman shrugged and cleared his throat.

"Sorry," he muttered. "I'd heard there was more than just a professional interest on your part in the Prescott woman."

Taylor added, "That's not smart and you know it, Myers. She might have been telling the truth about the savings account, but there's still a possibility she could be conspiring with her father."

"She's not." Caleb leaned forward casually and planted his elbows on the table. His voice was low-key, deceptively soft. "And whatever personal relationship we might develop is totally irrelevent to this case."

He looked both men in the eye. "My primary job is to assist you guys in finding out who's behind the virus program that aborted the Starseeker program. But it's also our responsibility to make sure that innocent bystanders—like Rae Prescott—are protected. If I can help in that capacity, I plan to do so."

"Take it easy," Taylor counseled. His weary, watery blue eyes analyzed and accepted the threatening aura emanating from Caleb. "No one's implying anything unethical about the Prescott woman or you."

He paused, then added flatly, "But you know we're going to

118

dig as deep as we can and follow up on every lead, regardless of the individuals involved. I want to agree with your assessment of her innocence, but until it's established beyond doubt, we can't afford to rule her out."

"I realize that." Caleb raked a hand through his hair. "Whose signature was forged—the brother's?"

"Yeah. He was pretty torqued about it. Especially when we had to warn him it might be his father."

"What did you learn about Ray Prescott, Senior?" Dennis asked.

Caleb produced the folded sheet from the inside pocket of his jacket. He handed it to Taylor. "A snitch happened to overhear a conversation in a bar between Prescott and an ex-employee of Chem-Con."

"That's the corporation that pirated, then produced the stolen Polaris technology in that case a couple of years back that you told us about, right?"

Caleb nodded. "It's my opinion that the same thing is happening with the Starseeker technology. IOS is after the money and power available for the sale of the technology more than trying to sabotage the country's security. T-bone—that's the snitch—overheard enough of Prescott's conversation for us to prove the IOS association."

Taylor lifted the paper, read it aloud. " 'I heard him tell the other dude that IOS better come through with the goods. The other dude told him to shut up and never mention the name. He looked around—I saw Prescott put something in his suit pocket. They left.' "

The three men were silent a minute.

"Prescott was sighted leaving a restaurant on Colfax last Tuesday," Dennis told Caleb. "We lost him at a traffic light. He hasn't surfaced since."

"Any more funds disappear from Rae's account?"

Taylor shook his head. "There's only about seven thousand left anyway. Prescott probably wouldn't risk an investigation by depleting the account totally."

Caleb stretched, then rose with a lithe coordination that belied the stiffness of his tired body. "I want to get back to the Springs. I have this uneasy feeling that he might try to implicate Rae again, somehow."

Taylor, his white shirt crumpled, the tie loosened at the opened collar, sighed and scratched the back of his head. "You could be right," he reluctantly admitted. "I talked to Ramirez earlier. They should have already tightened security around her."

"I'm going to drive on down tonight anyway."

"Are you crazy, man?" Dennis gaped at him in astonishment. "It's raining like the Last Flood, and it's long past midnight."

A corner of Caleb's mouth tilted. "I'll just have to hunt up a southbound ark."

Twenty minutes later, in an unmarked government car, he was headed south on I-25. Soggy with fatigue, eyes red-rimmed and grittier than ever, he still could not ignore the small but urgent voice inside, warning him of danger.

"Okay, Lord," he muttered as he squinted through the rain-lashed windshield and stygian blackness. "I'm going to need some help, or I'll probably end up at the morgue instead of my motel."

Less than ten miles out of Denver the rain quit, and a weak yellow moon hovered over the black masses of the mountains, lightening the midnight sky.

The sound of fire engines jerked Rae from a deep but restless sleep to heart-pounding wakefulness. An ominous reddish cast tinted the window shades; she stumbled out of bed, tripping over her slippers as she staggered to the window.

Cold, trembling fingers plucked aside enough slats to reveal one of her recurring nightmares of the past few months: her garage was on fire.

"The agents! Dear God, the agents hidden in the loft!"

120

She thrust her arms into her robe and crammed her feet into slippers. Even as she tore out the back door, the fire engine whose siren had awakened her rumbled to a halt. Men jumped off and ran over to the garage with their hoses unwinding across the lawn.

Forty minutes later it was over.

A pile of trash had been ignited with a kerosene soaked rag. Damage was minimal, except for the soot, ashes, and puddles of oily water. One of the agents—Charlie, she thought—had slipped her a note telling her not to panic. They were safe, and even if their stakeout had leaked somehow, they planned to remain until Agent Ramirez informed them otherwise. She was not to worry. This was just another scare tactic.

Rae thanked the firemen, reassured the police officer who had appeared that she was fine, and woodenly made a statement to the arson investigator who made out the report. Finally, she trudged on leaden feet back inside.

More out of habit than caution or suspicion, she made her way down the hall and unlocked the door to Joyful Noise to make sure everything was okay.

Everything wasn't.

All her ornaments, figurines, and music boxes had been hurled to the floor. They lay, mutilated and destroyed, in thousands of pieces. Only the brass quarter note remained unbroken, gleaming dully on top of the shattered onyx base.

Rae's fist lifted to her mouth, the other pressed against the top of her stomach, as if she were trying to keep her heart from leaping out. She shook her head slowly from side to side. "Father. . ." she whispered in an incoherent plea through numb lips, "help me. . .please help me."

CHAPTER 21

She had to call the police. Regardless of the consequences, she had to call the police.

Probably IOS would be waiting to see if she would do just that—there was a chance that if she *didn't* call, their suspicions would be even more aroused. What normal person with nothing to hide would fail to call the police when they had been viciously vandalized? But why just her treasures? Why had they destroyed all of them and left the music untouched?

She dialed 911 as if in a trance, and ordered herself not to even think about dashing back outside to the garage loft or the stakeout across the street.

She had to clear her throat twice before she could speak. "This is Rae Prescott," she told the bored sounding dispatcher. "My store, Joyful Noise, has been—" she stopped, biting her lip savagely until she had herself back under control. "My store has been vandalized."

The voice on the other end transferred her to the complaint clerk, who told Rae a unit would be dispatched to her address. Rae hung up.

Looking around vaguely, she automatically began checking the music bins. Some of the scores protruded; she carefully straightened, then pulled out a couple of pieces at random. Right then, destroying evidence was the last thing registering in her short-circuited brain.

Because she was hurting, she automatically drifted into the piano room and sank down onto the bench. Her hands arranged the music she had brought with her, then lifted to the keyboard and began to play.

She turned the page, and a folded piece of paper slipped out and floated to the floor.

Rae stopped playing and picked it up. Unfolding it, she glanced with indifferent curiosity at some meaningless notations. With a shrug, her fingers opened and the paper drifted back down to the floor. Rae didn't know what the notations meant or where the paper had come from. And she didn't care.

The police arrived just as she lifted her hands back to the keyboard, and she hurried with stiff gracelessness to the back door. Two cars, red lights flashing ominously, spilled forth what looked like an army of uniforms and plainclothesmen. One of them was Det. Grabowski: her faithful watchdogs must have notified him about the garage.

Across the street, she saw the DeVries's lights go on. Nancy had offered to stay with her after the fire, but Rae had managed to persuade her to go back home. The last thing she wanted was to be mothered like a three-year-old.

"Miss Prescott? Rae?" Det. Grabowski materialized at her side. He peered into her face, opened his mouth, then shut it. "Are you all right?" he asked after a minute, the normally hard, gritty voice was surprisingly gentle. He placed his hand on her arm and ushered her back up the porch steps.

"Not at the moment," Rae replied with ethereal candor. "I sort of feel like I'm not really here."

Grabowski jerked his head, then steered Rae out of the way. The lab technician and Evan McArthur, Lt. Grabowski's second-in-command, filed past. Another patrol officer loped across the lawn toward the DeVrieses. Hopefully he would be able to dissuade them from coming back over, along with asking them questions.

A female police officer, her rather rawboned, plain face softened by a pair of compassionate brown eyes, laid a comforting hand on Rae's shoulder.

"Why don't we go in the kitchen?" she suggested. "You can tell me what happened." She and Grabowski exchanged looks, but Rae was too insentient to notice their wordlessly communicated worry.

"What's the status on Myers?" Lt. Grabowski asked abruptly as he turned to follow the other men down the hall. He glanced from Rae to the policewoman. "He was scheduled to fly into Denver this evening."

"He hasn't checked in with us."

They both looked at Rae again. She stared sightlessly down the hall, seeing the shambles of her ruined treasures instead of walls. All the good memories she had so fiercely preserved over the last four years were destroyed, lying scattered in millions of pieces. And there was no one to turn to.

Uncle Floyd was dead.

Her brother Frank would say, "Good riddance. Now put the place up for sale and try to make a name for yourself as a concert pianist."

Caleb. . .she couldn't think of Caleb right now. If she even considered leaning on Caleb, she'd lose what little control she had left.

Rae shook her head in conscious denial, then slowly walked into the kitchen ahead of Officer Dix. Sinking onto the bench beneath the trestle table, she gazed down at her hands with unfocused eyes.

Up until a few months ago she would have proclaimed to the world her unshakeable faith in a loving God and thanked Him for His blessings. She had taken control of her life, made decisions, and never looked back. The seamy circumstances of her childhood could not touch her anymore, and she held her head high because she had created a fulfilling, satisfying lifestyle with her own two hands.

What had she done, for Him to allow these unspeakable circumstances that were crashing against the sturdy walls she had so carefully constructed?

"Miss Prescott? Rae? You look like you could use something to drink."

124

The kind voice penetrated her icy reverie, and Rae finally focused on the concerned face across the table. Her silver nameplate glinted in the light. Rae took a shaky breath. Standing, she walked to the stove. "Tea. I want a cup of hot tea. . ." she murmured through strangely anesthetized lips.

After fixing herself a mug of Earl Gray tea, she sat back down and looked vaguely at Officer Dix. "What did you want to know?"

Step by step she was led through the night's events, including the note Charlie handed her during the fire in the garage. When she choked, stumbling over words to describe the state in which she found Joyful Noise, Officer Dix calmly waited until she could continue.

Det. Grabowski entered as Rae concluded the dismal little tale. He walked wearily over to them. "They trashed your trinkets—but didn't touch anything else," he admitted musingly, and Rae flinched. "I wonder why. . . ."

"Apparently they started the fire in the garage as a diversion," Officer Dix stated. "Between all the hoopla over that, I guess neither of the feds in either stakeout caught the action."

"If the feds had been on the ball instead of joining the three-ring circus, we might have learned some useful information." Grabowski scowled at the toe of his scuffed black shoes. "Nothing could have been done to keep them from destroying the valuables, but at least we might have picked up a lead on the perpetrators."

Officer Dix shrugged, rose to her feet. "Can't say as I'd blame those guys too much. You know what a bummer pulling surveillance is. It's impossible to keep your eyes open every minute, even without a fire for a distraction."

Headlights flashed passed the windows, and into the sudden silence came the faint sound of a car door slamming. Officer Dix slipped her .357 revolver out of the belt-rig and moved swiftly in front of Rae. Det. Grabowski glided silently out into the hall, a 9mm semi-automatic appearing as if by magic in his hand.

125

Rae's heart, which until now had been lying in a cold, dead lump at her feet, kicked all the way up into her throat.

The back door burst open, and a man's voice echoed with sharp demand down the hall. "Rae! Where are you?"

Galvanized into action, Rae lurched upward, shoving Officer Dix aside as she hurled herself toward the sound of Caleb's voice. Later, much later she would have time to analyze, question, and regret the revealing response. But right now— "Caleb!" she cried in a broken voice.

His hair was damp, shaggy; his clothes were impossibly rumpled, and his eyes red-rimmed. In spite of obvious fatigue, danger and inimical threat emanated from him like a sizzling electrical current. He spared Grabowski one swift comprehensive glance, then turned to Rae who had fled into his opened arms without hesitation. Hands clutching the soft cotton of his shirtfront, nose buried in his chest, she at last allowed herself the luxury of relaxing her locked knees and pokered spine. Hot tears scalded her cheeks as she gave vent to the emotions held too long in iron control.

"What happened?" Caleb's voice, stripped for once of its low-key control, rumbled above her ear as his hands stroked her hair and shoulders.

"Store got hit by vandals, doubtless courtesy of your IOS pals. They trashed all her knicknacks—but left the music intact. We haven't yet determined if that was by accident or design."

Grabowski's terse explanation knifed Rae's lacerated nerves. She quivered, and the comforting hands tightened.

"Did the guys across the street get any pix? How about prints from your people?"

"They're just finishing up," the detective supplied with heavily exaggerated courtesy. "But no pix. A trash fire was set in Miss Prescott's garage to divert anyone who might have been interested in interrupting the 'party' in her store. The feds on duty all felt obliged to join the general commotion at the garage, ostensibly to offer help if needed." Grabowski's opinion of their actions hovered unspoken in the air.

There was a pregnant pause before he finished with pragmatic detachment, "Not that anyone would have interrupted even if the perpetrators *had* been seen. At this point we still can't afford to confirm the suspicions I'm convinced they're entertaining that Miss Prescott is under surveillance." He added softly, deliberately, "Or that she's planning a double-cross of some kind."

The cold, level words hammered into her body like individual blows. Rae's head jerked up and twisted around. "Don't. . ." she pleaded. "I can't—"

Caleb's hand slid around to cup her chin. He lifted her face and looked into her agonized eyes. "It's okay," he promised softly. "The most important thing is that *you* weren't hurt." His gaze burned into her. "The store might be your life—but it's not worth your life." One long index finger stroked down a tearstain from cheek to chin, then he realeased her.

The laser beam gaze transferred to a disapproving Det. Grabowski. "I brought back some information. I'll give it to you after I have a look at Rae's store, and you can fill me in on everything else."

Leaving Rae in her parlor, Caleb waved Grabowski down the hall ahead of him. He did not look at Rae again.

She stared after him; hurt and anger and bewilderment swirled around her like a swarm of angry bees.

CHAPTER 22

She sat in Uncle Floyd's favorite chair, waiting with growing restlessness. Officer Dix poked her head in briefly to confirm that Rae had nothing to add to her story and to remind her that they would need a list of all the destroyed valuables.

Rae nodded her head. Her fingers curled, the short nails biting into her palms.

Det. Grabowski returned and stood over her a moment without speaking, the light blue eyes speculative. Rae straightened her back and lifted her chin.

"I suppose you're wondering if I did it myself," she spoke in a remote, indifferent voice.

"The thought occurred to me. Every time I turn around lately, you seem to be in trouble of some kind. One can't help but wonder if it's designed to keep the spotlight on you—instead of where it needs to be."

She lifted her wrists. "Why don't you go on and arrest me, then? I might do something really dangerous the next time. Maybe I'm building a bomb in the basement. It's disguised as—"

"That's enough, Rae."

Caleb's calm voice cut off the flow of words. He walked across the worn Oriental carpet, warning Grabowski off with a single piercing stare. "What have you been saying to her, Grabowski?"

"Back off, Myers," the detective shot back testily. "I'll run my investigations the way I see fit—and you run yours. If I have to question Miss Prescott, I will."

"Maybe," Caleb assented, and Rae's temper fizzled and died at the latent threat icing his tone. "But while I'm protecting the lady, and it involves the Starseeker case, I'd recommend you keep your questions. . .polite."

"You wouldn't be threatening me, would you, Myers?"

Caleb smiled gently. "Not at all. That was just some well-intentioned advice."

Grabowski's brows lowered in a fierce scowl; then, abruptly, he gave a short laugh. "I'm getting too old for this," he muttered, shaking his head. "Have at her, son, but keep in mind what you've learned."

After Grabowski left, there was a moment of strained silence, then Caleb lifted Rae to her feet. She allowed that, but disengaged herself from his hands when she was standing.

"What have you learned?" she asked, not looking at him.

"Nothing good," Caleb responded. He lifted his hand, but froze when Rae flinched back. "Rae—trust me, please. It's going to be all right. I know you're not a criminal."

"Well, you're probably the only one." She swallowed hard. "What's the 'nothing good'? It couldn't possibly be any worse than what I've gone through tonight."

"That's why I think it would be best if you went back to bed. Things won't look so black later."

"Don't baby me!" she flared up, goaded beyond bearing. "I'm sorry I threw myself at you—believe me, it won't happen again." She watched with building wariness as flames licked through the amber eyes, turning them to hot, liquid gold.

"Yes, it will," he stated, his arms calmly wrapping around her and pulling her close. His lips brushed her ear. "Don't scratch, little cat. I'm wiped out—and seeing this place surrounded by squad cars aged me ten years."

He pressed light, soothing kisses along her neck and across her rigid jaw. "It was pouring rain in Denver, but I wrangled a car and came anyway. I *knew* something was wrong. I felt it. I prayed all the way down here."

She wanted to sink into the mesmerizing warmth Caleb offered. She wanted it with such frightening intensity her knees threatened to give way like dry sand. But every man in her entire life had always left her, and the risk was too great.

"I'm beginning to wonder if my prayers just sink through the

129

floorboards," she pushed against his chest, desperately turning her head away from those warm lips. "I must be doing something wrong for God to allow all this to be happening."

The caressing kisses stopped. He held her back, forcing her to meet his gaze. "You know better than that."

She felt color stealing into her cheeks. "It's gotten out of control, Caleb. Every time I turn around, something else happens. I feel so helpless, like my whole world was the house on shifting sand instead of the house built on rock."

A sob caught her by surprise, erupting from her throat. She blinked rapidly. "I had it all planned. Joyful Noise was finally making money—I'd done it. I had everything under control. Frank could eat all his hateful words. . . .I prayed so hard . . .thought God had answered all my prayers. . . ."

She brought a fist to her mouth, aware that she was coming apart inside and that if she didn't regain control, she was going to fly into as many pieces as her ruined treasures.

"Rae," Caleb's hands closed gently over her fists, the thumbs lightly running over her white knuckles, "God hasn't deserted you. Try not to question the whys, love. His answers just aren't the ones you were demanding. Instead, ask Him what you can learn from all this."

"I've learned I'm not any good at cops and robbers. I don't remember details; everyone but you suspects me of being in collusion with those despicable thugs, and I—I—" she closed her eyes against the tears threatening to spill over again, "—I want to crawl under the bed and hide. I never thought I'd be such a c-coward."

"Ah, Rae, you're no coward. . . ."

She felt his mouth again, this time on hers, his breath flowing so gently across her quivering lips she succumbed without protest. It was either kiss—or cry. Either way the loss of control was frightening, but the risk of revealing her deepening feelings for Caleb was still preferable to the humiliation of giving into the cowardly tears.

130

As long as he kept kissing her, she might be able to forget the shattering nightmare of the evening.

But she also had to face, at last, that she had fallen in love with a man who would disappear out of her life when the Starseeker case was eventually solved.

Karen was helping her clean the mess of her store the next day when the phone rang. Karen looked from where she was emptying a load of smashed glass into the trashcan to Rae, who stared at the phone as if it were a rattlesnake.

"You want me to answer it?" Karen asked, the drawl more pronounced than usual.

Rae gave a short nod. Caleb had called Karen last night and asked if she could spend the rest of the night with Rae. Alarmed, Karen had thrown on her bright yellow caftan and flown up the street, bursting on the scene like an enraged canary. Even Caleb, for all his phenomenal command of people, had needed a full fifteen minutes to calm her down.

Karen still thought setting up the SWAT team was a good idea. With a tired smile Rae had informed her that the Springs had a Tactical Enforcement Unit, not a SWAT team, and Karen should quit watching so much television.

All in all, Rae reminded herself now, her whirlwind of a friend had still been a welcome lifeline. She called all Rae's piano students and cancelled the lessons, insisting that the store be closed regardless of Rae's protests. She even handled the reporter from the *Gazette* after Rae's tenuous composure fractured, and she lectured the reporter on being nosy.

Rae nonetheless felt guilty about Karen's involvement. Her friend's voice would be picked up by the IOS phone tap. But it was too late now. Karen had answered the phone. "Hello. Joyful Noise."

There was silence as she listened, her extraordinary blue eyes widening, then narrowing. They slid over to where Rae stood, broom held suspended in her hand.

131

"Just a minute. I'll see." She put her hand over the receiver. "Rae, this man claims he's your brother. You want me to ask a few pertinent questions to confirm that?"

Rae gasped, and bumped her hip on the music bin in her haste to get to the phone. Just as she reached for it, she skidded to a halt. She bit her lip, thinking furiously. "Tell him I can't come to the phone right now. Tell him we're—we're leaving to go down to your place. If it's important, have him call me at the restaurant in a few minutes."

Karen looked absolutely baffled, but she relayed the message. "Okay, honey, give," she demanded after hanging up. "Ya got two minutes—then we have to boogie down to my place."

Rae stashed the broom and dustpan in the closet beneath the stairs. "Let's go. I need to get out of here." Her skin was crawling again, the oppressive awareness that her privacy was constantly trespassed closing over her in cold, lapping waves.

She told Karen about the bugged phone as they walked down the street.

Karen, with typical emotional fervor, shrieked in outraged incredulity. Rae found herself arguing fast and furiously before Karen finally agreed to keep her mouth shut. Rae shuddered to think of the implications if Det. Grabowski discovered Rae had revealed what he considered classified information.

Frank called five minutes after they climbed the stairs to Karen's apartment.

"What's going on?" he demanded irritably. "Why aren't you working in your store? It's ten o'clock out there, isn't it?"

"Hi, Frank." Rae's fingers absently played on the countertop where Karen's phone sat. "Why are you calling?"

A long-suffering sigh blew over the phone. "I wanted to make sure you were okay," he admitted. "Have you talked to the FBI about our esteemed father?"

Rae groaned. "Oh, Frank, this is the biggest mess."

"Tell me about it. I'm sitting in my office, fat, dumb, and happy, and some rock-faced fed in a three-piece suit lowered

132

the boom. I set up a savings account for you a couple of years back—didn't tell you 'cause I figured you'd try to dump it in that dumb house."

"Frank—"

He swept on, ignoring the stunned amazement in her voice. "Then this guy tells me that Dad did a doozy of a job forging my signature—and lifted all but a crummy seven thou from the account."

Rae felt the pain crusting in layers of ice. "*You're* the one who set up that account?" She closed her eyes, trying to assimilate the facts being dropped into her lap like sticks of lighted dynamite. "And our father stole. . ." her voice trailed away.

"You bet your sweet little bearish market," Frank shot back. "Look—haven't you talked to that Myers joker? I spent half the day on the phone with the FBI guys out in Denver, and then Myers rings me up at home a little while ago and rakes me over the coals for not telling you about the account. What's going on between the two of you, sis?"

Rae laughed—a hollow laugh. "I have no idea, brother dear. But I do know that if it hadn't been for Caleb, I'd probably be in jail now."

"Yeah, well, I guess maybe I should have told you about the account," he admitted awkwardly. His voice altered to a defensive, almost whining tone that catapulted Rae fifteen years back. "How was I supposed to know the old man would surface after all these years and have the gall to try some of his tricks on us?"

"Don't you start that old routine—" Rae began, then stopped. "Frank? Has he gotten in touch with you?"

"Are you kidding? If he tried, I'd have the old goat slapped in the slammer faster than the Dow dropped on Black Friday back in '87."

Rae nodded her thanks as Karen placed a mug of tea on the table beside the phone. She took a sip, then blurted out before she lost her courage, "Frank, did you know the FBI came to visit

Uncle Floyd once, asking about Dad?"

"Yeah—" he bit the word out, "I knew. I was fourteen—the guys had been hassling me about our background pretty bad. When two feds came, and Uncle Floyd told me to ride my bike to the store for a candy bar—I didn't."

Rae's heart went out to the sullen, rebellious teenager her brother had been. "Where did you hide? In that hidden pantry under the stairs?"

"Uh-huh. I heard an earful, too. They wanted him for transfer of stolen goods across state lines, larceny, car theft. . . ." There was a long pause before he added roughly, reluctantly, "I never told a soul, but I swore to myself that day I was going to leave and never look back. I was going to make a name for myself, and people would look at a Prescott with respect."

"I'm sorry, Frank," Rae said gently. "It was rough on me, too, even if I was too young to really understand. But it made such a difference when I—"

"Don't start all the Jesus stuff again. You know how I feel about that."

"I know. But I won't ever stop. I've got to keep praying that someday you'll be ready to listen. He helps, Frank. He really does." She wound the phone cord around her little finger; even as she spoke the words she felt a pervading peace and renewed strength flowing softly through her soul. "I don't have all the answers—and I've made a lot of mistakes—but in the past couple of months, I do know that if I hadn't had my faith in God, I wouldn't have made it at all."

CHAPTER 23

"Myers, we spend millions of the taxpayers' hard-earned dollars investigating people to avoid nonsense like the Starseeker sabotage. And now you sit there and tell me that this virus—this 'logic bomb' or 'time bomb' or whatever you called it—could have been planted in the software for over a year? It's unconscionable, man!"

Admiral Vale chomped on the end of a half-eaten piece of cinnamon stick candy. His narrow face was mottled red, his eyes hard as stones. Each word was spoken with pistol-cracking precision. "And I don't like it when you calmly warn me of the difficulty of getting hard evidence on this Fisher character."

Caleb continued to sit patiently, ignoring the smile Tray Ramirez was trying to hide behind his hand. "Sir," he pointed out when the admiral finally ran down, "you've been aware for two months now of the difficulty of tracing the source of the virus. It's only because of the elaborate security measures the joint services utilize that we've been able to narrow it down to Fisher."

He tried to placate the angry admiral with a reassuring smile. "My experience with these kinds of cases makes me feel pretty certain the virus had to be planted from the inside. There was little—if anything—your people could have done, Admiral."

"The military is trained to defend against *outside* aggressors," Tray reminded him, "Not insiders."

"I want the man picked up and dealt with now."

"You know we can't do that, sir. We haven't got enough concrete evidence to prove criminal intent, and without it, there's no hope of conviction."

"And may I remind you," Caleb continued with the blend of low-key authority and deference that kept the volatile admiral from erupting further, "that Fisher is merely a tool—the inside access IOS needed to achieve the sabotage? We're after the principals as well."

He looked straight across at the scowling man. "If we don't, they won't think twice about hitting on the military again. The next time, they might succeed with even more devastating results than the Starseeker sabotage."

"Impossible!" Admiral Vale snorted. "These programs are too complex, with too many safeguards—and they're closed systems. That's why we could put the finger on the little creep—as you just reminded me, Myers! We'll learn from the incident and adjust security measures accordingly."

With an abrupt, unconscious movement, his fingers snagged another cinnamon stick out of the jar on his desk. He stuck it between his teeth like a cigar. "I've talked to the chief of computer security for the Department of Defense. He sent his regards, by the way, and promised me you're the best."

He glared at Caleb as if wanting to question that assessment. "He also assures me that any further attempts would be detected and contained just as this one is, because of our technological control. We've also implemented a better password checker program and will be making more frequent data backups."

"Yes, sir," Caleb agreed. He did not point out that others weren't so assured about the inaccessibility, and that all discussions at this point were speculative, anyway. "But none of that negates the fact that Polaris might be out a contract. Both the Air Force and Polaris *are* out a considerable amount of money and wasted time. . .and IOS will continue to do as they please unless we find out who's behind this."

Admiral Vale slammed his fist on the table. "It's so frustrating! I feel like I'm on a destroyer trying to seek out and neutralize enemy subs—without sonar." He glared across at Ramirez. "Since Fisher is a civilian, I suppose that also means we won't be able to prosecute him under the Uniform Code of Military Justice. What *are* our options here, Tray?"

"The Attorney General will be trying for a conviction based on charges of harmful access to a computer." Ramirez leaned back in his chair and laced his fingers behind his head. "The State of Texas convicted a guy on that one last year, I believe."

He glanced across at Caleb, who nodded.

"And if there's any way to utilize the Computer Fraud and Abuse Act Congress passed in '86, they'll go for it."

The admiral heaved a sigh and chomped down on the new piece of candy. "I don't like all this clandestine maneuvering and namby-pamby political parleying." He quirked a thin gray eyebrow, his mouth curving in a wry half-smile. "Guess I've been a military man too long. When the enemy is identified, I want to go after him."

"I can understand that," Caleb murmured. He thought of his own feelings after seeing Rae's store the previous night. It was hard, sometimes, to remember that the Lord said vengeance belonged to Him.

"Tell me the latest info you've got," the admiral ordered abruptly, shrugging aside the momentary softening. "I have a meeting in an hour over at NORAD."

"We think at least two women are involved. No description yet," Ramirez supplied. "The Prescott woman happened onto what we think is an IOS identification code used by their female operatives."

"What about the Prescott woman?"

"She's a pawn," Caleb answered before Tray. "And nothing more. Her father's involved. So far we've been able to confirm that he's responsible for the funds used to pay off Fisher. He forged Rae's brother's signature, and retrieved the funds out of the savings account Frank Prescott set up without Rae's knowledge. The FBI have had a positive ID from the bank employee who gave Ray Prescott the money."

"He surfaced briefly in L.A. and Denver," Tray finished. "And Dennis Hoffman told me this morning that his car was spotted in San Francisco last night."

"At least the car he was driving in Denver," Caleb added.

"Do you think he's going to approach his daughter? Is that why there's been no evidence that IOS has moved the drop site?"

Tray looked at Caleb, who contemplated his hands with unnecessary intensity. "I don't know," Caleb finally had to admit, the syllables dragging out. He lifted his head, meeting the gazes of both men. "I'm afraid there is a very real possibility they'll try and frame Rae. They act like they're still not certain of exactly what she knows."

"What about Fisher?"

Caleb stood, a disconcerting restlessness crawling over him. "Fisher doesn't have a criminal mind. He's highly intelligent, but he's not devious. He's been collecting old sheet music for some time, so he doubtless feels comfortable going to Joyful Noise. There's a chance *he's* the reason the drop site hasn't been changed."

Caleb pondered the ceiling now, his eyes automatically noting even irrelevant details while his mind sifted and compiled information. "Maybe the guy just dug his heels in, and IOS, right now, has no choice but to comply. If so—or if Rae's father is framing her and IOS harms her in any way—then God help them both." His voice dropped to a sibilant whisper. "Because I'll track them down and nail their hides to the barn door, and that's only the beginning."

With the store closed for the day, and no piano students, time hung heavily on Rae's hands. After she and Karen parted, Rae indulged in a therapeutic bout of tears, cleaned her living quarters, then sat for awhile in Uncle Floyd's chair, reading her Bible.

Caleb's note had mentioned a Psalm—which one had it been? She could use—

The note.

Whispering a soft prayer of thanks at the jog to her addled memory, Rae dashed into her music room. Rummaging frantically through the music scattered on the floor, she at last unearthed the scrap of paper she was seeking.

Last night the meaningless jumble of symbols had been just that: meaningless. Today, with her equanimity at least partially restored, she could see another—alarming—possibility.

Rae's only experience with computers had been a class she had taken at Juilliard that taught a person how to compose music on-screen. It had been difficult but beneficial. And one day she hoped to have the funds to purchase a p.c. of some sort to use with her piano students.

She knew just enough computer language to recognize that the meaningless jumbles on the piece of paper were actually lines of computer code.

How had it found its way into a piece of her sheet music?

It could be just a worthless scrap of paper some customer had used to mark a piece. But perhaps one of those women who had worn the matching necklaces had accidentally dropped it while looking through the music. Maybe that's why IOS had been hounding Rae so mercilessly!

She had to take it to Caleb. He would know what the code meant and if it was significant. Gnawing her lip, she scurried back to the bedroom and hastily changed into clean clothes.

She folded the note into quarters and stuffed it in her purse. After a frowning moment, she dug it out and smoothed it into a slimmer half, then worked it deep inside the side seam pockets of her slacks.

Thinking in wild, furious bursts of strategy, she dashed to the garage and threw herself into her car. Her nose wrinkled at the heavy odor of burned wood, but she didn't spare a glance at the damage.

Forcing herself to drive with slow nonchalance, she stopped at a shopping center several blocks down Colorado Avenue. Hoping she looked like she was merely going to the grocery store, she hunted down a public phone in the back.

When she was certain nobody was within hearing distance, she called the number of the agents stationed across the street. "This is Rae Prescott," she announced breathlessly. "I need to get to Caleb Myers, fast. Can you tell me where he is?"

"What's the problem?"

The voice was unfamiliar and reeked of caution and wariness. Rae wanted to scream with frustration. "I think I might have found a clue," she hissed into the phone, her eyes sliding around furtively. "I've got to get it to Caleb. He'll know what it means."

"Miss Prescott, where are you calling from?"

"I'm not at home. I'm not stupid." Rae glared at the phone. "Look—I appreciate what you're doing, but this is important, and it doesn't need to wait until you guys can concoct some fancy little plan so I can pass this to you. Just tell me where Caleb is, and I'll take him the note!"

"I don't think that would be a good idea, Miss Prescott. Now, why don't you tell me—"

"Look—" Her temper snapped like pine kindling. "If you don't tell me where Caleb Myers is right now, I'm going to stroll across the street and announce to everyone who walks by just what's going on on the second floor of the old Selwyn home."

There were alarmed mutterings in the background, but she didn't care. She had to get to Caleb. She had to prove her innocence and turning this note over to Caleb could do that. He would *make* everyone see that Rae was innocent.

"Listen, Miss Prescott—" the conciliatory voice treaded with caution, "Mr. Myers is in a meeting out at Falcon right now. He, uh, he really can't be reached. If you—"

"Thanks! Radio whoever is supposed to keep a tail on me that I'll be headed east on Colorado." She hung up in the middle of the agent's urgent protests. She couldn't afford to listen, or she would be too terrified to do what she had to do.

She bought a bag of groceries for camouflage, not even aware of the items she flung hastily into the cart, or the strange look the cashier gave her at the checkout.

Traffic was light this time of the afternoon, and she made it to the east side of town with no trouble. But a three car accident at the intersection of Academy and Chelton snarled movement in all directions, and it took Rae a full ten minutes to finally maneuver past.

She hoped her watchdogs had caught up.

The road to Falcon Air Force Station wound through fifteen miles of almost treeless rolling prairie. Junkyards and occasional houses dotted the road at odd intervals, but at 1:30 in the afternoon, the road was deserted.

At least it was deserted until a huge black car roared up behind her and filled the rearview mirror. Rae glanced at her speedometer; she was already going sixty. Someone was in an even bigger hurry than she was.

She pulled over so the monster could pass.

The black car drew alongside her. Rae glimpsed a pale, sinister face staring straight at her with a ruthless, humorless smile. Recognition came a split second too late.

She jammed on the brakes just as the other car swerved, banging against the VW's front bumper and sending Rae hurtling in an out-of-control spin toward a wide, shallow ditch.

CHAPTER 24

Faces were bent over Rae and she felt hands touching her. She tried to scream and squirm away.

"Take it easy, Rae," a man's voice said. "You're all right. Just take it easy. . . ."

Something wet and sticky trickled down her forehead, into her eyes. She tried to open them, but it was like prying the lid off a jar of three-year-old canned preserves. She tried to lift her arm, but firm, restraining fingers closed around her wrist.

"Wait a minute," the same voice ordered. "Try to move your limbs slowly."

Something soft was pressed against her forehead, and she was tilted very gently back until her head rested against a seat of some kind. She finally succeeding in opening her eyes, and the first thing she saw was Det. Evan McArthur's concerned face. Beads of perspiration turned the deep chocolate skin a shimmering ebony in the bright afternoon sun.

"Hello," he said when he saw her eyes focus and register recognition. "Can you tell us what happened?"

Rae's head shook violently, and her entire body trembled. Pain slashed through her skull. "I—I ran off the road," she whispered through constricted throat muscles.

"How's she doing?"

J.W. Ayer, his clever, good-looking face shadowed with worry, appeared behind Evan. The light gray eyes moved over Rae. "I radioed Falcon—Myers is on his way, but I don't think we better wait. She looks like she's in shock."

"Pulse is shallow, rapid—but I think I got the bleeding stopped on her temple. She might be concussed, but there're no broken bones, at least."

J.W. leaned forward suddenly, a frown deepening when Rae

flinched back. "Look at her throat. Does that look like something the shoulder strap would have done?"

Rae shook her head. She lifted feeble hands to push them away. "No. . ." she protested, her voice alarmingly weak. "I'm fine. I ran off the road." Her vision blurred, and the words suddenly seemed too large to escape her mouth. "Ran. . .off . . .road," she repeated, as the two faces swam in front of her, then slid down a long black tunnel.

"She's scared of something. . . ." The voice came from a distance.

"Yeah—whaddaya think?"

"I think we should get her to the hospital, and hope Myers can find out what it is. That guy could pry the pearl out of an oyster and have the oyster thank him."

"Maybe so, but I have a feeling we're gonna be in deep Dutch with both him and Grabowski for letting her get away from us."

"We're not responsible for the Springs traffic. . . .It's a bad scene all the way around, man."

The last pinprick of light vanished, and the men's voices were drowned out by buzzing bees swarming in Rae's head. She moaned an incoherent protest, then gave in to the bees.

The next time she regained consciousness she was lying on a gurney, with a sheet covering her from the neck down. Antiseptic and ammonia smells stung her nose, and there was a continuous murmur of voices and scraping footsteps from behind the light green curtain drawn around the cubicle where she lay.

Slowly, cautiously, she opened her eyes and turned her head.

"Rae. . ." Caleb's large, warm, infinitely gentle hands enclosed her face, and his lips touched her brow. "How are you feeling, love?"

"Caleb." She tried to smile, but her eyes filled up with tears.

143

He wiped them away with the backs of his hands.

"Easy, easy. You're okay. Bruised, slight concussion, and tomorrow all your bones will probably let you know about the battle you lost with a ditch. . . ." His voice suddenly roughened, and the fingers lightly skimming her face trembled. ". . .But you're okay. Thank God you're okay."

Rae lifted her hand to his. She slipped her cold, trembling fingers inside, warmth flooding her veins at the comfort and strength of his touch. If anything happened to Caleb. . . .

The curtain billowed as Agent Ramirez, Det. Grabowski, and a man Rae had never seen crowded around the gurney.

"Can you answer some questions for us, Miss Prescott?" Agent Ramirez asked.

A harried nurse elbowed her way through the cluster of men. "Look, guys, I know you want some information, but the lady doesn't need to be disturbed."

The man Rae didn't recognize took the nurse's arm, murmured something, then led her outside the curtain. Rae's eyes moved from Caleb to each of the men. Caleb's hand tightened reassuringly. What could she do?

"Miss Prescott," Ramirez continued, his voice gentle, but his eyes determined. "We know you were coming to Falcon to see Myers. We've listened to the tape," he added, and Rae closed her mouth.

"She's hiding something," Grabowski said sharply. "You can see it in her face." He whirled to Caleb. "Myers—"

"Back off. Give her a chance." Caleb looked down at Rae, his expression communicating nothing but encouragement.

Rae started to shiver uncontrollably. She didn't want him defending her, shielding her. Not now. Not when it could cost him his life.

"What did you find, Rae?" he asked. "It must have been pretty important, right?"

Rae stared at him dumbly.

"Miss Prescott—Rae—have you been threatened again?"

144

Det. Grabowski asked. "Or was chasing off toward Falcon with a supposed clue a diversion of some sort?"

"Grabowski—"

Rae squeezed Caleb's hand. "It's all right," she said. She lifted her eyes to the detective and held his gaze without flinching. "I did find a clue." Her voice was soft but firm. "It looked like lines of computer code, and I wanted Caleb to see it because I knew he would know what it meant."

"We searched your car, Rae," Agent Ramirez inserted. "There was no sign of a note." He paused, then added, "The contents of your purse were scattered all over the front seat and the floorboards. I guess the impact threw everything out, hmm?"

Rae felt three sets of eyes burning holes in her, and she wanted to dive under the thin sheet. Thank God she had had the presence of mind to put the paper in her pants pocket. But was it still there?

She felt Caleb's fingers brushing aside the beads of perspiration that had popped out on the unbandaged side of her head.

"Was the note in your purse, Rae?" he asked quietly.

Rae carefully shook her head. "I put it in my pocket." With slow movements, her free hand searched beneath the sheet. Her fingers touched the paper. The relief was so overwhelming she knew it must show on her face. All three men leaned forward, the tension twanging inside the small cubicle.

She withdrew the crumpled note and gave it to Caleb.

He unfolded it, and one eyebrow disappeared beneath the errant lock of hair that always fell over his forehead. "Well, well, well. . . ." Bending, he pressed a soft kiss against Rae's cheek, then straightened and turned to the other men. "Gentlemen, I think the case is about to break."

He handed the note to Tray Ramirez. "If I'm not mistaken, what Rae found is part of the commands from the Starseeker program."

145

He might as well have pulled out an M-16 and sprayed bullets in the ceiling.

"Are you sure, man?" Stunned, Grabowski looked from the note to Caleb, then down at Rae. "Where did you find this, Miss Prescott?"

"It was in a copy of a Brahm's sonata." Rae could not comprehend the magnitude of her inadvertent discovery. "The one in F minor. Opus Five. I was just playing scores at random after my store was vandalized." She kept her eyes on Caleb, unaware that the gaze was almost pleading. "The note fell out. It didn't make sense at the time."

She swallowed, wishing she could have a drink of water. "I just kept on playing. . . ."

"When did you realize it was more than just a random piece of scrap paper?"

That was Agent Ramirez. Rae forced herself to look at him, and surprised a glimmer of compassion beneath the maddening blank wall look all the agents seemed to have perfected.

"Earlier. . .today. . .I was reading my Bible." She glanced up at Caleb, a faint blush just staining her bleached countenance. "I remembered Caleb had mentioned a verse from Psalms in the note he left for me, and that was when it suddenly hit me that that piece of paper—" she nodded toward the note, "—might be more than just a scrap some customer had used to mark a piece of music."

"Where's the music it fell out of?"

Rae felt the blush deepening into temper at Det. Grabowski's tone. She could tell he didn't really believe in her innocence. "It's still on my piano," she replied, frost coating the words. "The minute I realized it might be a clue, I left the house and called the agents to find out where Caleb was. If I was planning a double-cross, or I was a member of IOS—or any of all the other perpetually suspicious ideas you've formed about me—I would have destroyed the note, not tried to find Caleb."

She tried to sit up, wincing, resisting Caleb's hands when they

146

pressed against her shoulders. "Well?" she shot at Det. Grabowski. "Can't you bring yourself to admit you were wrong about me?"

"Easy, Rae." Caleb leaned down, and his breath nuzzled her ear. "Your claws are showing, little cat. Just try to relax."

"I admit that your explanation and actions are plausible," the detective returned slowly, but his blue eyes were narrow, speculative. "But I'm still waiting for you to tell us why you're frightened. According to my men, you tried to fight them off even before you were fully conscious, and there have been several times these past few moments when you've been evasive."

He crossed his arms, head back as Rae quit struggling to sit up and collapsed limply back onto the gurney. "How 'bout it, Miss Prescott? If you'll come clean, maybe then I won't harbor all my—um—nasty suspicions, shall we say, about you."

Fists clenched, eyes closing in desperation, Rae scrabbled frantically in her mind to find a way to avoid the implications. Her head throbbed in protest, and she opened her eyes. "Can I have some water?" she asked weakly. "I don't feel good. . . ."

"I'll ask," Caleb replied. He shot a commanding look at the two men. "Let's talk outside."

He left, the tilt of his head and shoulders an unspoken demonstration of his assurance that his order would be obeyed.

Rae lay with her eyes closed, her body shivering in reaction. When the clucking nurse appeared with a paper cup of water, Rae's hands were trembling so badly, the nurse had to hold the cup to her lips.

"I should never have let that silver-tongued guy bamboozle me," the nurse muttered. "They've gone and upset you, haven't they?"

"It's just all catching up with me," Rae said as she thanked her for the water. The nurse helped her sit up, and Caleb came back into the room.

"Now she needs nothing but peace and quiet—"

"That's what I'm here to insure," Caleb interrupted with a lopsided smile that hushed the mothering nurse instantly. "I've talked to the doctor. He assures me that it's perfectly safe to release Miss Prescott. I'm taking her home."

Without quite knowing how it happened, less than ten minutes later Rae was comfortably ensconced in the seat of Caleb's government-loaned car, and Caleb was driving through the rush hour traffic.

A few minutes later her startled gaze flew to the rearview mirror. "You missed the turn to my house," she protested, fighting to keep the alarm out of her voice.

"I know," was the calm reply. "Lean back and rest, honey. We're just going up the road a little ways." The car stopped at a traffic light, and he turned toward her, capturing her in an inscrutable study that turned the light amber eyes to the mesmerizing gold of a tiger's eye. "Then you and I are going to talk."

CHAPTER 25

Bright afternoon sunbeams shot over the top of Pike's Peak into the valley below, reflecting off the incredibe slab-like red sandstone formations of Garden of the Gods.

Caleb turned onto the road leading into the park entrance, and drove along the winding lanes until he found a deserted spot to pull over. He helped Rae out, then without speaking, lifted her into his arms and began walking.

She was stiff, her eyes as dark and turbulent as a captured doe. He smiled down at her. "I thought this would be a good place to talk," he shifted her a little to navigate around some jutting rock and scrub oak.

The road behind them disappeared. He swiftly surveyed the area, and when he neither saw nor heard any sign of other people, he carefully deposited Rae on a patch of dry ground. After kicking aside a couple of stones and some twigs, he dropped down beside her.

"I've been coming here a lot the past months," he admitted, lifting his face to the warmth of the sun. "It's so peaceful, but so larger than life. It puts this whole tangled up case in perspective and helps me think."

Rae glanced around indifferently. "What did you want to talk about?" she asked with obvious reluctance.

He turned and looked directly at her, noting the determined jut of her chin, the long narrow nose, the freckles only now fading back into creamy skin that had regained a little of its color. Her eyes.

She was so transparent, and he was in love with her. "I want to tell you what I've found out about your father," he said quietly, pain twisting his heart at the knee-jerk reaction his statement triggered. Then she bent her head, turned so that all

149

he could see was the shining mass of hair, arranged in a chignon that was lopsided and slipping loose.

Before he could help himself, his hands lifted to pull out the pins. "What are you—Caleb, stop!" Her hands tried to slap his away.

"It was falling anyway—and I bet letting it down helps your headache." He touched her bottom lip with his finger. "Doesn't it?"

Her shoulders lifted in a shrug. "I really am going to cut it all off one of these days." She gnawed on the lip he had touched, making him want to cover her mouth with his and stop the revealing action.

"Caleb?" She was looking at him now, the gray eyes fogged with shame and worry. "What did you find out?"

Caleb sternly pulled his thoughts back to the matter at hand. "He's one of the IOS couriers," he admitted without dressing it up. "As well as playing the part of front man and engaging in grand larceny and any other schemes to provide extra funds." He laid his hand over hers which had clenched into a fist. "Your father is the one who stole the money out of that savings account, Rae. I'm sorry."

"I know. I talked to my brother."

"Mm-mm. I suppose you got an earful, since I hadn't had a chance to get back and explain after your store was vandalized."

"It was a shock," she confessed. "But nothing worse than what I've suspected for years. Uncle Floyd refused to talk about him at all, and when I'd question my brother, he'd get this horrible scowl and just tell me to shut up. By the time I was fifteen, I figured I'd be fortunate if he wasn't wanted for murder." She looked at Caleb, her eyes swimming. "I know it's not supposed to matter when I'm a Christian, Caleb. But it does. . . ."

With an inarticulate groan, he turned, wrapping her in a close, protective embrace. "I'm sorry, so sorry." He kissed the top of her hair, then pressed his cheek to the soft strands. "I can't identify with your agony, Rae—but I can share the burden."

He clasped her shoulders, then held her a little ways from him. "I think one of the reasons you're so strong now is because of what you endured as a child. I guess that's part of what Paul is talking about in his letter to the Romans, when he tells us all things work together for our good—when we love the Lord."

"I don't feel very strong right now." Her fingers fiddled with the buttons on his shirt, then dropped to fumble nervously in her lap. "I feel more like I've been strapped into an out-of-control roller coaster." She tried to smile. "It's a shame there's not a piano close by."

"Is that how you release tension, get back a little of the control you feel like you've lost?"

She looked startled at his perception, and Caleb smiled to himself. "I suppose. I've never really thought about it that way, but you're right. I do feel like I'm in absolute control when I'm playing the piano, which is sort of ironic. My professor told me the only time I ever looked relaxed, lost almost, was when I finally mastered a piece and knew where I was going with it."

"How'd you get involved with music, anyway?" Caleb turned her so they were sitting comfortably side by side, with his arm still holding her close.

"There was an old upright in the parlor. I used to bang on it. After Mother died, Uncle Floyd would hold me on his lap and pick out tunes. He told me it was the only way he could get me to smile."

She looked out toward one of the massive red formations, her gaze unfocused. "He got me started on lessons, and the teacher said I had a good ear. Uncle Floyd, partly because he was an indulgent, impractical old man, and probably partly out of guilt for the mess his brother had made of our lives, decided I deserved only the best."

She sighed, stretched her hands out and examined the long, slender fingers, the short, stubby nails. "So I ended up at Juilliard, with the promise of a fairly successful career after I won a couple of competitions. But my finances were in a mess, and ultimately, saving the Prescott family home mattered more than a career. It's the only *decent* legacy I have."

"Most people with your opportunity would have kissed the place off without looking back."

She shrugged again, a measure of tranquility returning to her face. "I did a lot of praying about it. I just felt Uncle Floyd deserved better than that. He took us in, gave us everything, tried his entire life to make us feel like a—a family, tried to make up for what our father and mother were."

She looked up at Caleb. "I don't regret it. I receive enough satisfaction when I see the faces of our congregation after I play a stirring offertory, or when one of my students finally masters Beethoven's *Fur Elise* and realizes the poetry in classical music."

Caleb cupped her face in his hands, caressing the fragile cheekbones with his thumbs. "Y'know something, Miss Rae Prescott? I think you're one special lady—regardless of your family ties."

Her eyelids drooped and her lips half-parted; Caleb could feel her trembling response. Totally unable to stop himself, he lowered his head and kissed her. Her unguarded reponse licked through him like a flaming sword. "Love," he whispered eventually, kissing the translucent eyelids, the narrow nose, "we've got to stop this and talk."

"I don't want to talk. . . ."

But the white bandage covering her forehead was a vivid reminder of the menace still lurking in the shadows. He pressed his hand to her cheek until she opened her eyes. "Rae," he said, very gently, "I'm afraid your life may be in danger because of the Starseeker case and your father's involvement with IOS. So far, I think they've been playing with you, waiting to see if you could be used. But finding that computer code changes everything."

152

He wouldn't let her look away. "I don't think you were meant to find that, but because you did, I also don't think IOS is going to be playing with you anymore." He took a deep breath, searching her widening eyes. "Will you tell me now what happened when your car went off the road? You didn't lose control, did you?"

She shook her head in agonized denial, pulled free of his hold, and staggered to her feet. "Caleb. Don't ask me. Please."

Standing there, her hands in fists by her sides, her luminous gray eyes eloquently pleading, it was all he could do not to sweep her back into his arms, then spirit her off to the sanctuary of his parents' Florida home. He leaned back, propping on his elbows, and watched a hawk lazily circling above them.

"I can't protect you if you don't level with me," he remarked with feigned casualness.

"I don't care about me!" she burst out suddenly. "It's you. You!"

He picked up a piece of straw grass and twirled it idly. "What do you mean?"

"I can't tell you anything because of what might happen to you," she stormed. "They said—" she stopped abruptly.

"Who said?" he repeated, rising lazily to his feet and regarding her steadily. "Who, Rae?"

She shook her head again, so violently that she winced from the pain, and her hands flew to her bandaged head. "I can't!" she moaned. "Caleb—they'll kill you."

"And do you think they'll stop with bruising your throat the next time—or just running you off the road?" He saw his educated guess hit home, and a slow burning rage he had never felt in his life gathered force deep inside. "Who was it, Rae?" he asked, his voice very level, very quiet.

Rae backed a step, goosebumps cropping up on her arms in spite of the heat of the late afternoon sun.

"They ran you off the road, didn't they?" He stepped toward

153

her. "And then they threatened you—warned you to keep quiet?"

Rae stood statue still. "One of them started to choke me when he couldn't find anything in my purse," she said in a flat, dead voice. "The other one made him quit. Then he said they'd kill you if I tried to identify them. He told me nobody ever double-crossed IOS, and if I tried, I'd lose more than a few lousy trinkets."

The gaze she turned to Caleb made him take her back into his arms. He pressed her head against his chest, fighting to control the trembling rage. "I heard the siren from J. W.'s and Evan's car about that time, but I guess I passed out." Her words were muffled against Caleb's shirt.

"Rae. . ."

Her arms snaked around his waist and hugged like a limpet. "If anything happened to you, I couldn't bear it," she choked out in a desperate, broken voice. "I couldn't."

"How do you think I feel about you?" He lifted her head, gazing deeply into her eyes. "Rae—little cat's claw—" the words welled up and spilled out before he could stop them, "I'm in love with you."

Incredulous, incandescent joy flooded her face. Jeweled tears sparkled as her hands slid from his neck to touch his mouth, his jaw. "Caleb. Oh, Caleb. . .I love you, too!"

He caught her close, lifted her and twirled her around, murmuring incoherent words and phrases.

"God sure has a funny sense of timing," he observed a long while later, when the first euphoric joy had calmed to a steady, brightly burning flame. "I've known since the first time I saw you that you were different, special—but I was on a case. I kept trying to ignore the feelings, and telling Him I didn't understand why you stuck in my mind like a puzzle I couldn't solve."

Rae giggled and rubbed her face against his neck, below his jaw. "It was your eyes that got to me. Nobody's ever looked at me quite the way you did—the way you do."

154

"And nobody *but* me better do it in the future." He kissed her soundly again. "I've prayed since I was in my late teens that God would provide my mate, my perfect helpmate. But after so many years, I'd about decided that wasn't part of God's plan for me."

"I'm not perfect, Caleb," Rae felt obliged to remind him. "I have this temper, if you'll remember—and I'm absentminded and non-observant except with music, and I—"

"And I love you the way you are, warts and all." Caleb hugged her. "Now—before it gets dark and we get lost trying to find the car—can we finish the conversation that's ended up a whole lot differently than I anticipated?"

"Are you disappointed, Mr. Myers?"

"Don't be cute, Miss Prescott." His hand brushed over the bandage. "But it has suddenly become even more important to me to see to your safety and continued well-being."

"No more so than yours," Rae shot back.

The sun vanished behind Pike's Peak, throwing their world into darkening shadows. Caleb, his mood altering almost radically, took Rae's hand. "Let's go get something to eat," he said, "and we'll try to come up with a plan of action."

Chapter 26

After a dizzyingly circuitous route that carried them over most of Colorado Springs, Caleb drove through the gate at Peterson AFB. Rae looked around, never having been on a military base before. At nighttime, there wasn't much to see but streetlights and the blurred outlines of buildings.

Caleb watched her with secret amusement. "Not exactly what you pictured?" he queried after a few minutes.

She returned his grin sheepishly. "I guess I thought it'd look more like a communist outpost or the Berlin Wall or something. You know—miles of barbed wire and marching men and guards with machine guns."

"And the only guard you've seen is the gate guard with a 9mm Beretta, and he smiled at you."

"Well. . .at least all the buildings look blank and undistinguished and—military."

"Undistinguished or not, and regardless of the smiling guard, the security at this base is tight. Don't be fooled into thinking that just anyone could stroll past that smiling guard, or drive onto the grounds for a casual picnic."

He was silent a minute. "I've really come to appreciate the sacrifices these people make the past couple of months. I also appreciate Admiral Vale fixing things so we could set up another field office here."

His gaze rested on her a moment. "I don't worry as much about walking you into an ambush on a military base."

They pulled to a stop in front of a low building with few windows. Caleb kissed her as he helped her out of the car, then ushered her inside the building and down some depressing-looking corridors and through a doorway.

Tray Ramirez, Joe Drexel, and Chuck Livingston, two other

156

FBI agents, looked up from a table. Their frowning faces lightened a little. "Sit down, Miss Prescott." Agent Ramirez pulled out a chair. "You look a little better than the last time I saw you."

Color blossomed in Rae's cheeks, and Caleb suppressed a laugh. He winked at Rae as she sat down. "Fresh air'll do that for you, won't it?"

Once everyone was seated, all levity vanished. The agent handed Caleb a folder; he scanned the contents and his mouth tightened.

"Rae," he asked, watching her carefully, "remember when you told the Springs detective—J.W.—about the two women who wore matching necklaces?"

Rae nodded.

"I know you were unable to provide a physical description, but would you try again? For me?"

The other agents leaned forward, their intent expressions betraying their heightened interest. Caleb knew they made Rae nervous, but it couldn't be helped. "Close your eyes if you think that would help," he offered.

Rae obeyed, but after a few moments of painful concentration she opened them again, and spread her hands ruefully. "I think the young one was blonde—and I remember smelling cigarette smoke around the other one. But beyond that. . ."

Joe casually flipped over a black and white snapshot and slid it across the table. "What about that?" he asked. "Does that jog your memory at all?"

Rae picked up the picture and studied it. "The face is familiar," she allowed slowly. Her nose wrinkled, and Caleb found himself wanting to kiss it.

"When and where?" he gestured to the photo.

"Denver, outside the bank where Miss Prescott's account is. The man has known IOS connections. The woman was followed back to the Springs where she met Fisher in a local restaurant."

157

"Did they exchange anything?"

Ramirez scowled. "We don't know. They were sitting at a booth, and we weren't able to snag a table with a view that would allow us to monitor any transactions."

Rae was still studying the picture. Caleb glanced at her, then continued talking in a low voice with the other agents. Tray was able to confirm that the note Rae had found was, as suspected, two lines of the Starseeker commands. Archie Cohen, Tray added sourly, had raised unholy havoc when Tray refused to release the note into his custody.

"Wait!" Rae grabbed Caleb's arm. Her voice was vibrating with excitement. "Look—see the bag she's carrying? The photo's black and white, and that's why I didn't notice at first, but the more I looked—"

"Rae. . ." Caleb laid a calming hand over hers, "what is it?"

"The bag—it's from Joyful Noise. It has the big treble cleff on it, just like my car!"

Tray exclaimed softly, triumphantly, and Joe and Chuck pounded the table. "We've got them," Tray announced. "We're gonna nail 'em."

At Joyful Noise, business resumed as usual. Rae's customers commiserated over the loss of her treasures, and her students continued to hate scales and arpeggios. There was no sign of a woman wearing a unique thunderbird necklace.

Rae tried her best to memorize details of everyone who came in, but even with her heightened senses, all the customers looked and acted prosaically normal.

"I mean," she was chatting with Caleb over supper at the Gibson Girl one evening a week later, "it's so absurd trying to imagine one of them trying to pass government secrets. I have a regular customer—he was in today, as a matter of fact."

She dug into the spinach salad Karen had just placed in front of her with a smile and wink. "He's shy and retiring—collects old and out-of-print classical sheet music, if you can believe it." Chewing, she grinned across at Caleb, who was watching her with an alert, arrested expression. "Can you imagine someone like *that* being involved with IOS?'

"Was he looking for anything special today?" Caleb asked casually.

Rae shrugged, took another bite. "He did ask me to keep my eye out for a particular edition of Mendelssohn. Come to think of it, I need to give him a call. Some woman called just before the store closed. She wants to sell a bunch of music from an estate sale."

Caleb leaned forward, his gaze so intent Rae blushed.

"Do I have dressing on my nose?" she asked, swiping at it with her napkin.

"Your nose is covered only by freckles. Do you think the Mendelssohn might be in the music that woman wants to sell?"

"I know it is," Rae answered matter-of-factly. "I asked her, she searched, and actually found it. I thought it was really great, and told her I had a customer who was going to be very happy. Isn't that a marvelous coincidence?"

"I—" Caleb stated very softly, "—don't believe in coincidence." He spoke with such latent menace Rae dropped her fork. It clattered on the plate as she gaped at him, open-mouthed and puzzled.

"Caleb?"

He leaned over the table, his eyes swiftly scanning the nearby diners. "When did this woman say she could get all the music to your store?"

"This Saturday." Rae bit her lip. "It wasn't a coincidence, was it?"

Caleb shook his head. The ginger-ale eyes, so warm and tender when they looked at her, were cool now, as hard as polished pebbles. "No, love, it wasn't a coincidence."

But that means Mr. Fisher. . ." her voice trailed away, and she shook her head in denial. "Caleb, he's so *timid*. He can't be involved."

"Your timid Mr. Fisher is one of the programmers who designed Starseeker. And he's also the one who's been selling the technology to IOS, a piece at a time. Yes, he's nervous, probably even scared. But he's shrewd, greedy—and after revenge."

Rae shoved he salad aside, her appetite gone. "Then was he the one who left that note in my music? The note with the computer codes?"

Caleb nodded. His hand reached across to pat hers. "We've suspected Fisher for months, but I didn't want to tell you because I was afraid you wouldn't be able to act normal around him." He squeezed gently. "You're much too honest to be successful with deceit, my love.."

"I thought I was doing a pretty good job playing secret agent." She glanced around, lowered her voice. "Caleb—the music. He's using the music, isn't he?"

He nodded, looking pleased and alarmed all at the same time. "Tray and I suspected as much last week, after you told me where you found the computer code. Hoffman and Grabowski agree with me. We've been racking our brains trying to think of a way to prove it, to catch Fisher and his IOS contact passing the information.

Suddenly he stood up, pulling Rae with him. "Let's borrow Karen's apartment. I don't like talking in here. Will she mind?"

"Not at all."

Karen bustled over in response to Rae's slight wave. Caleb spoke to her in a low voice, and after a delighted peal of laughter, Karen waved them through a door at the back of the restaurant. She promised to bring the rest of their meal up on a tray as soon as she had a free moment.

Up in the apartment, Caleb motioned Rae to a chair. He then placed a call to Tray after making sure Karen's phone, and the apartment, were free of any uninvited 'bugs.' Rae watched in silent stupefaction.

"I think Rae stumbled onto the system," he spoke in his low, easygoing voice, but Rae detected the underlying excitement. "Fisher asked her to be on the lookout for a particular piece of music. Several hours later, Rae got a call from some woman wanting to sell a pile of old music, and one of the pieces just 'happened' to be the copy Fisher's after."

He listened a minute, glanced across at Rae, and smiled reassuringly.

"Yeah, I know. All we have to do is catch 'em passing the info. But if my hunch is correct, Tray, this will be the big one. Things have gotten too hot, especially after Rae happened onto the code he was supposed to pass onto IOS. What?"

His brows tightened together, and the knuckles of the hand gripping the receiver turned white. His head swiveled toward Rae, who watched him with love, concern, and remnants of incredulity still reflected in her eyes.

"That makes it even more likely that they're winding it up, and IOS will hand over the big pay-off. What? This Saturday? Yeah, I know. I don't either." He raked a hand through his hair. "It's risky, but I think you ought to put some people on the second story, over the store."

His mouth tightened. "I want to catch them—all of them— just as much as you do. But I will not allow her to be placed in that kind of danger."

Rae stood, crossed over, and wrapped her arms around his waist. "Caleb, don't—"

He laid firm fingers over her mouth, cutting off the words. "Tray, we can discuss it later, at our usual time. You can get hold of the others—you might give Grabowski and the Springs intelligence unit a call as well. I'll see you in a couple of hours." He hung up.

"I won't let you wrap me up in protection like a baby in a blanket," Rae immediately announced. She pinched the hard muscles below his ribs.

Caleb looped a long arm around her waist and picked her up like a sack of groceries. "What I won't do is allow you to be set up; your life placed in jeopardy." He deposited her at one end of Karen's Victorian fainting couch, and sat down next to her. "Rae, your father was spotted in a bar down on Platte last night."

The hands she had lifted dropped limply in her lap. "What are you saying?" she asked after a moment, her voice carefully stripped of feeling.

"He acts like a mailman for IOS. If he's here, it's either to pick up the Starseeker technology, or to bring in the rest of the money IOS is paying Fisher. Maybe both."

He dropped another kiss on the tip of her nose. "Rae, I want to put you on a plane and send you down to my folks in Florida until this is over. I don't suppose you'd consider it?"

"No way," she breathed, the determination in her eyes plain to see. "No way on earth will you get me away from here. I'm involved because of my father and because of my store, and I'm seeing it through to the bitter end."

She ran her fingers through the lock of hair falling over Caleb's brow. "Jesus could have called an entire legion of angels to set Him free. I figure maybe, if both of us ask, God might choose at least a couple to protect us from trouble."

"Rae—"

This time she stopped his words with her fingers, ignoring the tingling sensation shooting down them when his lips kissed the sensitive tips. "He might," she finished almost desperately, "surround us with songs of deliverance, like the psalmist says in Psalm 32."

CHAPTER 27

It was even harder trying to live a normal life when Rae knew there were two men stashed upstairs, figuratively looking over her shoulder and breathing down her neck.

Even when she knew they were there to protect her, as well as to trap the traitors, she found it almost impossible to relax. For the first time in years, playing the piano didn't help. Too aware of the reason for her unseen audience, Rae could not lose herself in the music.

Consequently, her temper simmered and bubbled, rumbling beneath the tissue thin surface charm she fought to project to the world. More than once she also had to fight to keep from dashing outside and screaming at the top of her lungs, then climbing in a car and driving until she ran out of gas.

She couldn't even pray coherently beyond a constant plea for God to keep her from exploding into a million pieces.

It was a gray, chilly day for the first week in May. Instead of sunny skies and mild temperatures, winter winds whipped around corners, plunging temperatures into the forties. Sullen clouds slogged over the mountaintops, and the smell of rain hovered in the air.

The store bell jangled, the wind almost tearing the heavy oak door out of Mr. Fisher's hands as he entered the shop. Wisps of mousey hair were tangled all over his balding head; his nose and ears were pink with cold. "Not much of a spring day out there," he greeted Rae.

Rae's smile was more a baring of teeth. She had spent the better part of three days mentally rehearsing her behavior for the next time she saw this man. In her unstable mood right now, however, she felt more like grabbing the collar of his expensive looking silk shirt and giving him a shaking. "No, it's not," she settled for a terse response and avoided making eye contact.

Mr. Fisher rubbed his hands together, darting surreptitious looks around the store. "So—how's business been lately? Had any more excitement around here?"

Rae jerked, unable to hide her startled response to this supposedly innocent *non sequitur*. "Uh—no. Nothing. Having the entire collection of birthday gifts my uncle gave me destroyed has been excitement enough." *Not to mention abduction, threats, and a few other ho-hum events not worth mentioning. . . .*Fortunately, she clamped her mouth shut before she, in fact, *did* mention all the trials for which the man in front of her was directly responsible.

"Oh." Mr. Fisher smiled a sickly smile, the sallow complexion emphasizing the sharp bones of his face, the prominent Adam's apple. He glanced toward the still bare shelves, just visible through the doorway. "I heard about—I mean a friend of mine who came—" he floundered to a halt, finished with stuttering desperation, "You, uh, you say my Mendelssohn will be in tomorrow?"

"Yes." Rae pretended to look for something under the counter so he couldn't see her face. *Get out of here, please,* she begged him silently. If he hovered much longer, asking questions like that, Rae was terrified she would say something she wasn't supposed to.

"What are you doing?" he asked sharply, and Rae's head jerked up with a snap.

Music, Joyful Noise sacks, and her ledger cascaded to the floor. "O-ooh. . ." Rae pressed her fists against her temples.

"I'm sorry." Mr. Fisher hovered, hands flapping uncertainly. "Here—I'll come around and help pick—"

"No!" Rae interjected, then tried to soften the word with a smile. "I'll do it. You go look around. Was. . .was there another piece you were looking for, like the Mendelssohn?"

He turned pasty white, and behind the thick glasses his eyes blinked rapidly. "Why did you ask?"

"No reason. I—I just wondered what you were doing here." She closed her eyes in frustration, hating herself. "I mean—I mean you don't usually come on Fridays. . . ."

He began backing away, his eyes flickering around as if he expected the boogy man to jump out at him. Or worse. "Look—I'll come back another time. Tomorrow. It's obviously not a good time for you. . ."

Shoes clattering on the warped oak flooring, he tugged open the door and rushed down the steps. Chill tendrils of wind licked over Rae from the slowly closing door.

With her bottom lip clenched between her teeth, she picked up the mess on the floor. Heavy foreboding congealed in her stomach like cold oatmeal. Mr. Fisher had been as jumpy as Rae; now the whole Starseeker case teetered on the edge, inches away from collapsing on top of both of them.

The phone rang a little after four. It was the woman who planned to bring in all the music from the estate sale. She told Rae she wouldn't be able to come in after all.

"Oh, please—" Rae burst out across the woman's good-bye noises. "Mr. Fi—I mean, my customer will be so disappointed."

Frantically, she cast about her stampeding wits to come up with a more persuasive argument. Her mind spat back nothing but jumbled phrases.

"I'm sorry," the cool voice on the other end was saying. "Tell your customer maybe another time."

"Listen—where do you live? I could come pick the music up."

There was dead silence from the other end.

Rae's hand was slippery with sweat, heart slamming against her ribcage. "I really wouldn't mind," she pressed, praying for a calm voice. "I did promise I would have the Mendelssohn on Saturday, and I hate to go back on my word."

"Just a minute."

The phone was covered, and Rae could hear nothing but the somber ticking of the mantel clock over the fireplace—and her own erratic breathing.

"Can you be here at four o'clock?"

Rae wiped her palm on her slacks. "Where do you live?"

"If you can't be here by four o'clock, your customer will just have to be...disappointed. I have an engagement elsewhere."

The woman was obviously not going to provide directions until Rae agreed to the time. "I can be there by four," she answered slowly, reluctantly. *Caleb, forgive me.*

There was another crackling pause, then the woman issued a set of sharp directions. Rae's heart swelled in a crescendo of rolling fear.

"If you're not there by four," the curt voice ended, "you'll have made the trip for nothing. I have to leave by five after."

"I'll be there."

"I don't care if you plan to bring in the National Guard. It's too dangerous. She's bait for a trap. You know it. I know it." Caleb snagged Rae's eyes in a brief, searing glance. "Even Miss Prescott knows she's been set up."

The conference room throbbed with tension. Not only were Caleb, the FBI, and Det. Grabowski present, but a deputy investigator from the El Paso County sheriff's office as well. For the past twenty-four hours, Sgt. Benthall and Tray Ramirez had been coordinating the deployment of people, studying maps and photographs—and planning.

Nobody really wanted to use Rae. She was a civilian. Caleb was not alone in his reluctance.

Det. Grabowski said it best. "Only exigent circumstances allow this," he finally ground out. "I can't think of another case with these unique conditions, but right now I don't see that we have any better options."

Dennis Hoffman crossed and re-crossed his legs. Long and lanky, he looked more like the center for a basketball team than an FBI agent. "He's right, Myers." He also leveled a look at Rae,

166

one that spoke of frustration and disgust. "This is our only chance to nail them now, and you know it."

Rae wrapped her fingers around the chipped ceramic mug one of the agents had scrounged for her. "Caleb, since it's my fault Fisher spooked, it's up to me to make amends."

Just then, Caleb did something she would never have dreamed he was capable of doing. He picked up an ashtray full of cigarette stubs and hurled it across the conference room. It slammed against the wall, rending the air with the sound of shattering glass. Then he slammed his palms down on the table, and the look he leveled at Agent Hoffman was so fierce, hairs stood up on the back of Rae's neck.

"Rae's a civilian," he enunciated with deadly softness. "Regardless of her feelings to the contrary, she is *not* responsible for fouling up the case. And Hoffman—" he leaned over until their noses were only separated by inches, "I'd appreciate it if you'd stop playing on her guilt and concentrate your mental faculties on coming up with an alternative plan."

Frozen into silence, the clutch of men in the room stared at Caleb; Rae carefully put her mug of lukewarm tea aside and rose. Moving as if she were approaching a cornered wild animal, she sidled over to Caleb.

Laying tentative fingers on his bunched shoulder muscles, she peered up into the iron mask of his face. "Caleb," she spoke his name in a low, firm voice, "you can't put the blame on Agent Hoffman or anybody else. I volunteered. I *choose* to do this."

Caleb didn't turn his head. "You've done enough, Rae. You've had enough done to you. I want you out of it. Now."

"Caleb," Rae repeated with the same underlying steel, "you don't have the right to give me that order."

"Myers, we'll have—"

Dennis Hoffman made the mistake of meeting Caleb's unrelenting gaze—and closed his mouth.

Rae moved back, breathing slowly and deeply to maintain

167

control. If she pretended she was about to walk across the stage to perform, she could stay calm, give the illusion of perfect control. If she looked into Caleb's furious eyes like the hapless agent had done, she'd collapse like a split sack of sugar.

"I'm going to be wired," she reminded him now, "and there will be undercover cops and agents positioned all over the place." Her mouth flickered in a half-humorous smile. "About like fleas on a stray dog from what Sgt. Benthall tells me. I'll be all right, Caleb."

"We don't *know* that." He straightened, breathing hard. "There are so many variables, so many things that could happen beyond our control."

"Then," Rae murmured, looking at him how with eyes full of love, "we'll just have to depend on the One who is always in control, won't we?"

His head jerked around, and all of a sudden his shoulders slumped. Dropping into the chair, he closed his eyes as his hand pressed against his temple. After a minute, he looked over at Agent Hoffman. "I'm sorry, Dennis," he apologized quietly. "I had no right to behave that way."

Sighs of relief rippled around the room.

"Don't worry about it," Hoffman waved aside the apology. "We're all concerned about Miss Prescott. But unless she goes to supposedly pick up that music, the Starseeker case is dead in the water. We can't prove Fisher left the program in the music, we don't even have a positive ID on the woman who seems to be controlling him—and the whole case wouldn't stand a chance of making it into court."

Caleb looked up at Rae at last. "I know," he answered, his gaze asking forgiveness, betraying fear, admitting defeat. "God help me, I know."

CHAPTER 28

She drove south on I-25 toward Pueblo in her borrowed car. To her right, rolling hills and water-chiseled ravines covered with scrub and a few trees provided training grounds for Ft. Carson. To her left, a winding ribbon of cottonwoods lined Fountain Creek. On that side the terrain was flat, with few hills. Few places to hide.

Beneath her loose knit top the velcro holding a thick belt with its tiny, sophisticated transmitter in place tugged Rae's skin. She ignored it. Her hands gripped the steering wheel with single-minded ferocity; her eyes watched for landmarks.

"Don't worry. We'll already have everyone in place by the time you show." That had been Sgt. Benthall. He had smiled at her, a gold-capped tooth flashing. But the dark brown eyes had been watchful, flat.

She had driven almost ten miles now. The exit should be coming up soon.

"Just be as natural as possible, Miss Prescott. If she gives you a stack of music, thank her and leave. If she dreams up some excuse for not having it, smile and thank her, no matter how implausible the excuse is. . . ." That had been Agent Ramirez, looking serious and grim, his suit jacket tossed aside to reveal the ominous shoulder holster with the ugly butt of his gun protruding.

There. That was the exit the woman told her to take. Rae flicked on the blinker and turned. Sweat rolled down between her shoulder blades, dribbled down her temples. She turned left, crossed over the freeway, then turned onto a dirt road paralleling I-25.

She noticed a car tucked under the overpass, almost lost in the shadows. Releasing a quivering, pent-up breath, Rae tried to sing. Her voice warbled as she realized how many men would be

169

picking up the sound of her voice, and she shut her mouth.

There. A dirt road winding east toward Fountain Creek, with smatterings of cottonwoods on either side. She drove under the railroad tracks, dust billowing out behind her in a choking cloud. Yesterday's rain had never materialized.

Rae didn't see any other cars, and almost panicked at the thought. She had already noted the troubling fact that there were few places to conceal men and cars in this relatively flat area. Where could everyone possibly hide?

"Rae, just remember to keep your temper—stay cool." That had been Caleb, his golden eyes bathing her in loving concern. "They might suspect you of all sorts of schemes—but they don't know for sure, so they'll wait for your behavior to clue them."

He had tapped her nose, then held her hand between both of his. "I'll pray not only for your safety, but that God will give you self-control. And don't forget all those guardian angels that will be surrounding you. . .since I can't."

He had muttered the last, frustration lashing the words. Rae wanted to close her eyes to better picture her last memory of the man she loved, but the road was too narrow and curving.

Taking a deep breath, she drove carefully around a bend between a stand of cottonwoods and oaks. Off to the right, almost hidden in trees, nestled a run-down house with a "For Sale" sign leaning drunkenly in the front yard.

"I'm coming up on the house," she murmured. Officer Dix had promised that Rae's voice—and any others within twenty feet—would be picked up. Hidden somewhere in the area, inside an innocent looking van, Rae knew every word would be faithfully recorded.

The stubborn lump in Rae's throat ballooned to the size of Pike's Peak when she turned into the front yard—there wasn't a driveway—and turned off the ignition.

The house looked deserted. A sagging front porch, dingy, peeling paint. . .screen door with the screen ripped halfway out—the place fairly screamed, "This is a set-up, Rae Prescott!"

Rae squared her shoulders and lifted her chin. "Though, tum-de-dum—an host, tum-de-dum—encamp, tum-de-dum—against me. . . ." She sang beneath beneath her breath, her gaze on the two windows. They stared back, like two blank eyes covered with black patches.

She marched toward the rickety porch steps. "My heart. . . shall not fear. . ." *If anyone believes that, Lord, I'm a better actress than I thought.*

With icy fingers that barely felt the rough wood, she dragged open the screen door and knocked.

The door was yanked open so suddenly Rae's hand stayed poised in mid-knock. "Hello," she said. "I'm Rae Prescott, here for the music?"

Through the roaring in her ears and the suffocating pounding of her heart, Rae felt an inexplicable sense of calm wash over her. She might have just delivered herself into a den of lions, but power and confidence flooded her veins. She hadn't felt this kind of exhilarating high since she sat down on the bench to play in a competition at Carnegie Hall.

Five years ago she had walked off with first place.

As she stared into the face of a tall, dark-haired, dark-eyed woman, Rae had a feeling this time might be different. Especially when her eyes fell to the necklace around the woman's neck.

Rae's mouth dropped open, and her eyes opened wide. "The necklace!" she exclaimed with unforgivable witlessness.

The woman's eyes narrowed to slits and her breath escaped in a hiss. "I knew it," she breathed, clamping surprisingly strong fingers around Rae's wrist and dragging her into the room. "You *did* catch on. You've been playing a game of your own all along, haven't you? Who's your contact? Where's the note you stole out of the Brahms?"

Rae opened her mouth, but the other woman silenced her with a curt motion of one ring-laden hand. Her narrowed eyes glittered like shards of onyx.

"It's been tried before," she swept on, the words hissing

171

snake-like between thinned lips. "But no one cuts in on my turf. No one." Her gaze raked over Rae. "So you thought you'd steal Starseeker for yourself, hmm? Thought your two-bit innocent act would fool me?"

Hot color flooded Rae's face. She wrenched her arm free and stepped back. "I didn't steal anything! I came here to pick up some music," she said, fighting to stay calm. She wet her lips, swallowed. At what point *did* innocence become stupidity? "I recognized your necklace—it's beautiful, and I think I told you so the first time I noticed it in the store."

The woman hesitated, studying Rae as if she were an unfamiliar insect crawling across the floor. Rae was sickeningly afraid that her attempts to bluff her way free weren't going to work.

Without taking her eyes off Rae, the woman spoke again. "I think she's lying, Jim-baby. Why don't you come on out and see what kind of reaction we get?"

There was silence, then the sound of footsteps scraping hollowly across the bare floor in another room. When Mr. Fisher's stoop-shouldered form shuffled into view, Rae's eyes widened. She couldn't help it.

He looked at Rae in sheepish apology and quaking fear. "I'm sorry, Miss Prescott. I never meant—"

"Be quiet! We've got to find out how much she knows before—" she stopped, slanted Rae an unpleasant, feline smile, then finished with calculated cruelty, "—before we clean house and disappear."

"Larissa, wait a minute." Mr. Fisher's face was a sickly green, and the eyes behind his glasses glinted with liquid fear. "You promised me no one would get hurt. And I *have* brought the rest of the non-contaminated program. Let's just leave her and go."

Larissa whirled on the hapless man like a snake. "Shut your mouth, you fool!" She peered out the curtainless window, fingers drumming on the dusty ledge. "I knew I shouldn't have given in to your whining. If we'd moved the drop like I suggested, this could have been avoided."

She speared Mr. Fisher with a look of chilling contempt. "But you had to 'feel safe.' You wanted—you *insisted*—on using that stupid store. What happens now is all on your shoulders, Jim-baby. Remember that."

Rae decided to take advantage of the distraction. She edged backward, trying to keep her face expressionless.

She saw Mr. Fisher glance at her, then hurriedly away. Larissa snapped back around. "You're not going anywhere." Rae stopped, paralyzed by the flat menace in her voice.

"Look," Rae spoke as soothingly as she could, trying to pretend she was Caleb, conscious of the listening ears beyond the walls of the house. "Whatever you're doing is obviously illegal, and I don't appreciate your using Joyful Noise, but if—"

Larissa's face changed. "Don't threaten me, honey. If it hadn't been for your old man, you'd have been out of the picture weeks ago." She watched Rae, then laughed an ugly laugh. "Yeah, that gets you, doesn't it? Your father thought you might be a useful tool, Miss Prescott. And for awhile, he was right."

Thrusting her face right up to Rae's, she laughed again. "Your father," she repeated. "How does it feel knowing he doesn't care this much—" she snapped her fingers under Rae's nose, "—about you?"

"Larissa," Mr. Fisher pleaded uneasily, glancing at Rae's face.

"If I hadn't been so suspicious that he might be using you to pull a double-cross on me, those two 'visitors' at your house would have done a lot more than threaten you." She moved casually behind Rae and blocked the door. "So. . .why don't you just tell me how much you *do* know?"

"Why don't you tell me what you've been passing back and forth in my sheet music?" Rae countered, dropping all pretense of ignorance. Larissa's calculated barbs hurt, but Rae would not let them devastate her. She had something far more urgent on which to concentrate: her life.

Mr. Fisher's face turned a mottled red. "You *have* known. Miss Prescott, I thought you were a nice person. . .I even felt sorry for you, because—" He stopped, shooting Larissa a frightened, sulky look.

Rae regarded him incredulously. "You use my store to pass stolen information, jeopardize national security, throw my father's involvement in my face—and now you're upset that I know—that I won't close my eyes to the whole affair?"

"It's the government that's not fair—and that smug, pompous, Jackson Overstreet!" Fisher glared, his Adam's apple bobbing with nervous little jerks.

"Fisher—"

He ignored Larissa. "Sitting on his millions, taking all the credit—well, not this time. This time *I'll* have the money, the prestige. *I* will." He turned to Larissa then, his eyes pleading. "Won't I, honey? Just like you promised? And I did bring the last of the program with me. Your boss won't have any reason to doubt now. Let's just leave Miss Prescott and go."

Larissa's laugh this time echoed in the dingy room like crows cawing over a carcass. "That's right, Jim-baby. Leave her here to blab everything to the feds. They've been sniffing around you for a month now, trying to pin some evidence on you."

Fisher swallowed hard. "I don't care what she's done. I don't want anybody hurt."

"You'll look real spiffy in a prison suit."

Desperation flooded his face. He looked like a trapped animal; the wild, calculating eyes flickered from side to side as though trying to find a bolt-hole.

Rae didn't move. She could feel the knife-edged danger that hovered in the air, and knew her life hung in the balance.

Against her waist, the velcro on the belt scratched, providing a modicum of reassurance. Rae's hand moved involuntarily to cover it, then dropped back to her side.

"You won't have to watch," Larissa was saying acidly. "Jules and Romo will take care of it. All you have to do is deliver her to the address I'll give you." Her voice rose impatiently. "Oh, quit looking like such a rabbit! Did you honestly think I'd leave behind any tale-telling mouths? That's not our way, Jim-baby."

She took a step toward Rae. "We can either do this the easy way, or I knock you out." She stared at Rae with flat, indifferent eyes. "I have a brown belt in karate, and none of your religious scruples."

Rae faced her with calm dignity. She had already determined not to put up a fight; in the process, they would inevitably discover the transmitter. Rae's last hope of rescue lay beneath the folds of her sweater. She held up her hands.

"I've been beat up on enough," she admitted.

"I always did admire someone who gives in gracefully," Larissa murmured, stepping closer. "Jim-baby, there's a rope in that closet. Fetch it for me like a good boy."

"Miss Prescott, she means to have you killed!" Mr. Fisher exclaimed hoarsely.

"I didn't think she wanted to play jump rope," Rae managed to retort through a cotton-dry mouth. She would not give in to the fear rolling over her in wave after deadly cold wave. She would not.

Larissa grabbed her arms and wrenched them behind Rae's back. Rough strands of rope were wound about her wrists, then her ankles, the coarseness biting into tender skin. Rae bit her lip and prayed, focusing on the window and the world beyond. Somewhere out there a lot of men knew what has happening. They would rescue her before it was too late.

Caleb would rescue her.

She smiled at Larissa. "You might think I've given in gracefully," she announced calmly, "but you're wrong."

Larissa snorted. "I'm never wrong. Don't think you can bluff me, you sanctimonious little nun."

"You were wrong the first—no, the second time you came in my store. In fact, it's because you were wrong that you're in a whole lot more trouble than you think."

Larissa's hand shot out and fastened in Rae's hair, yanking her head back painfully. "What are you talking about?"

Tears pooled, but Rae gave back look for look. "You don't know the first thing about music," she shot back. "You proved that when you asked for *Ode to Joy* from Beethoven's Fifth Symphony."

She heard Mr. Fisher inhale sharply.

Rae managed to maintain a serene smile in spite of the stinging pain in her scalp. She gazed directly into the furious eyes inches away from her own. "The *Ode to Joy* is from Beethoven's Ninth, Larissa who-ever-you-are. You were wrong about that— and you're wrong about me."

"How could you be so stupid!" Mr. Fisher raged, almost jumping up and down. "This whole thing is your fault! Yours! That's why the code wasn't in the music that time. That's why you had to send those two goons back and ended up with the police and the feds on our tail. That's—"

"Shut up!" Larissa shoved Rae at the raging man, almost causing both of them to fall. "Just take her to this address and get out of here! I'll take the program."

Staggering beneath Rae's trussed, dead weight, Mr. Fisher cast the other woman a frantic look. "My money!" he whined. "What about my money?"

"It will be deposited after my people run a test on the whole Starseeker program." Her voice dripped acid. "You better take care of *her*, exactly like I've told you—or you won't be around to spend it, Jim-baby."

Suddenly she moved across, thrusting her face right next to Rae's one last time. "Say your prayers, honey. And regardless of which stupid symphony that song came from, I guarantee you won't be interested in any odes to joy where you'll be going."

This time Rae's smile didn't have to be forced. "Wrong again, Larissa. You're wrong again."

CHAPTER 29

"We have to pull her now." Caleb grated the words. Fear coiled in his stomach, a timber rattler poised to strike. "You heard what Fisher said. They're going to kill her."

The stark words hovered inside the murky confines of a dusty cream-colored van, where he, Tray, and one of Benthall's men had been listening to the grim little performance taking place a few hundred yards away. They exchanged glances, then with one accord Caleb and Tray snatched up a couple of binoculars and jumped out the back doors.

Crouched and alert, they made their way to the front of the van, then crawled to a position where they could see the house.

"We've gotta get her out now," Caleb insisted again. A muscle in his jaw twitched.

Tray did not move from his position on the ground, keeping his eyes glued to his binoculars. "Cal, you're losing it, man. You know we can't make our move yet. It's going down—and we have a fighting chance of nabbing more than just Fisher and the woman." He shifted slightly. "You stick with Fisher, okay? You can follow along, then move in with the others before he transfers her."

Caleb, lying beside him, dug his fingers into the dry dirt, crumbling it to dust. A pebble dug into his left hip, but he barely noticed the discomfort. *Father, I can't stand this.* "Tray, we're not talking about a professional agent here. Rae's a civilian. She's not trained to handle—"

He saw the corner of the FBI man's mouth lift. "I'd say she's done pretty good. You heard her—we should be able to get a conviction on attempted murder as well as theft of classified technology, thanks to Miss Prescott's presence of mind. She's got a lot of class, Cal."

Caleb was proud of her, too, but he knew Rae better than Tray did. She might sound calm, in control outside—inside he knew she trembled on the verge of collapse. *Stay close, Lord. To both of us. . . .*

It was impossible to relax. Lying belly-down in the dirt beside Tray, sweat dribbling down his forehead, Caleb struggled to keep his hands steady on his binoculars. Every muscle in his body was violin string taut.

Tray's radio crackled. "They're leaving," he muttered.

Caleb watched, grinding his teeth, as the door of the ramshackle house opened. Fisher and the woman manhandled Rae across the barren, stubbled yard.

Caleb jerked, his teeth snapping together with an audible click. The powerful binoculars brought Rae's face as close as if he were standing right in front of her. It was contorted in pain, the fear bleaching her colorless face. He watched her bite her bottom lip to keep from crying out.

A tall, dark-haired woman impatiently pushed at her. Fisher staggered, threw the woman a whipped-dog look, then tumbled her into the back seat of Rae's borrowed blue Cutlass. The woman mouthed a terse comment, her face a mask of impatience.

Rae, Caleb screamed silently. *Rae. Hold on.*

He half rose, muscles bunched and ready. Tray's hard hand pushed him back down, his voice brusquely reminding him of the need to stay concealed.

Fisher climbed into the driver's seat. The woman slammed the door, leaned over the open window a moment, then turned and strode rapidly toward a shed half-hidden behind a stand of willow oaks as Fisher drove recklessly away, a billowing cloud of dust marking his route.

Tray spoke into his hand unit. "Suspect headed west in victim's car, a two-toned blue '83 Cutlass. License plate Kilo, Uniform, Hotel, three-seven-seven. Suspect driving."

A black Corvette pulled out of the shed with Larissa behind the wheel. It tore down the dirt road in the opposite direction.

Caleb and Tray scrambled to their feet. Tray spoke in the radio again, reeling off the direction of the Corvette. Binoculars dangling, fists clenching and unclenching, Caleb watched the two departing cars with strangling impotence.

"Get moving, man!" Tray snapped beside him. "We've got tails on them both, so get hold of yourself."

The words were as effective as an electric cattle prod. Caleb tore off down the gully at a dead run, fear, rage, and helplessness pumping through his body in a roaring red tide.

The cars had shrunk to miniature toys, the blue Cutlass weaving with drunken haste toward I-25, stretching in front of them like a dusty ribbon. In their wake, rolling clouds of dust wafted gently toward the two running men.

"I haven't seen you this wired since we met," Tray observed between breaths as they sprinted back down the wash to the spot where they'd left their cars. "You're always so in control."

Caleb's heart was clawing its way up his parched throat. He couldn't speak as he dodged around a clump of tumbleweed. *Father, please don't let me be too late. . .please. . . .*

About a hundred yards south, they joined the other agents, Benthall's men, and the Springs intelligence guys.

"Did you copy everything?" Tray asked them.

Dennis Hoffman nodded. "Fisher's headed back toward the Springs. Benthall's unit will pick 'em up when they hit the freeway. The Corvette's headed south—I've got another car on her tail. Benthall alerted the units in Pueblo." He allowed satisfaction to coat his voice. "I think we got 'em."

"Until Rae Prescott is safe, nothing is finished," Caleb spoke between clenched teeth as he wrenched off the binoculars and tossed them to Tray. Hoffman's premature, self-congratulatory aura grated. "I'm going after Rae. I want to be there when Fisher tries to dump her."

"Stay out of it, Myers," Benthall warned. "Your part in this is over. It's our business now."

Caleb ignored him. He bolted for his car, hidden in the cottonwoods growing thickly along the creek. "That's what you think," he growled.

He didn't wait for Tray or the other agents. Throwing himself behind the wheel, he turned the ignition with a savage twist, then gunned off down the rutted path that led back to the dirt road.

Rounding a curve, topping a rise—there was Rae's car, gathering speed as it headed up the entrance ramp to I-25. Caleb watched the cops stationed beneath the overpass pull out, climb the embankment, and pursue Fisher at a discreet distance.

Caleb speeded up, jarring his car over potholes and bumps with reckless disregard for the vehicle's shocks or chassis. He passed under the railroad, and the freeway was just in front of him. He had to get to Rae. *Hold on, little cat's claw. I'm coming. Lord, keep her safe. Please.*

With a roar and squealing of tires he rocketed up the ramp. An eighteen wheeler was approaching in the near lane, but Caleb shot in front of the cab with just feet to spare. He ignored the warning blast of the truck's airhorn.

Traffic going toward the Springs was heavy; he dodged cars with fierce concentration, barely able to restrain his foot from flooring the accelerator. This was no time to have an accident— and he could not endanger innocent people. Rae. . .Rae. . . .

He forced himself to remember that the car was being closely monitored. Fisher wouldn't be able to lose the squad cars that would be in active pursuit once they hit the city limits. Caleb's eyes restlessly surveyed the road ahead. There! A flash of blue.

Scenery passed in one continuous blur while time crawled. Two minutes slipped by, then six. He grabbed his radio. "One-x-fifty-one to one-x-fifty. Request position of suspect vehicle."

"X-fifty. . .vehicle entering city limits. Maintain positions."

He was too far back. The car gathered speed, the needle

creeping past seventy. Almost ten minutes had passed. He topped a hill just in time to see the Cutlass exit at Nevada.

Caleb's heart jerked once. He noted with abstract astonishment that he was sweating like a racehorse, even though the temperature was holding in the low fifties. Unbearable scenes of past cases, where the good guys had been minutes too late, the bad guys seconds too soon taunted his mind with each agonizing minute.

He also saw a pair of gray eyes filled with love, with joy. They blurred, blackened with fear, with screaming terror.

"Father, no!" he groaned aloud.

He came to the exit, hurtled down it too fast, and screeched to a standstill at the bottom behind a bright red Cherokee. Up the heavily traveled street, the car with Rae in it turned right and disappeared.

Caleb grabbed the radio again. "X-fifty to x-forty-seven. Request immediate intercept." Protocol be hanged. He wanted Fisher picked up *now*. Which patrol units were covering this sector? McArthur and Ayer, he knew, were the detectives. He also knew they drove a white hatchback Mustang. Where were they?

He was forced to wait agonizing seconds as an endless stream of cars chugged past, all with the speed of a dying snail.

The radio crackled. "X-forty-seven. Suspect turning right on—" Static garbled the transmission, but not before Caleb caught a bitten-off exclamation.

He had finally turned onto Nevada and was speeding up the street, one white-knuckled hand on the wheel, the other clenching the ominously silent radio. By the time he made it to the street where Fisher had turned, it was too late. But he saw the white Mustang that had pulled over to the curb. Pulling up behind, he jumped out of his car, and sprinted up to join Evan McArthur and J.W. Ayer. "What happened? Where's Fisher?"

"Get in with us, man!" Evan slapped a fist-sized portable siren-bubble in place while J.W. spoke rapidly into the radio.

181

Caleb barely had time to slam the door before they tore off in pursuit.

"Fisher did an illegal U-turn—practically got wiped out by a truck," McArthur threw over his shoulder. The detective's face was grim, savage. "They stopped in front of an alley, another car pulled up, and a guy jumped out. He grabbed Miss Prescott, tossed her in the back of their car, and took off."

"They're headed west on Colorado," J.W. added. He spoke into the radio again. "Responding code three—we're westbound on the avenue and attempting to intercept suspect vehicle. Request code one and assistance."

J.W. twisted his head around and caught Caleb's eye. "She'll be okay," he promised, trying without much success to sound confident. "There're at least four units responding, not to mention your people."

Caleb nodded grimly. He watched the stores and cars and people pass by in a tumultuous blur; his fingers fiddled helplessly with his watchband. Rae. . .Rae. . .

Terror yapped and nipped at Rae, circling her like a pack of frenzied pit bulldogs as hard, urgent hands grabbed her out of Fisher's car and threw her into another one. Rae squirmed, then opened her mouth to scream. The attempt ended in a choked gasp when her head struck a glancing blow on the door handle.

"Get moving," a dead-fish voice ordered. "The little chip-head's sure to have brought company."

Rae knew that voice, knew she would hear it in her sleep the rest of her life. Fighting dizziness and nausea, she struggled to sit up, to see where they were.

The tall man, who days before had run her off the road then throttled her, smiling all the while, turned and smiled at her again. "You don't learn, do you, Miss Prescott?"

If I throw up now, I'll just die, Rae thought, then giggled hysterically. She *was* going to die—if Caleb hadn't managed to stay up.

She struggled to work free of the ropes, focusing her mind, her thoughts. "You'll never be a world-class pianist if you don't focus, Prescott," her professor at Juilliard used to say.

The Apostle Paul said he could do all things through Christ...if she focused, maybe she could free herself from the ropes.

"Cops!" the driver suddenly hissed frantically. "Where'd they come from? What'll I do?" Panic coated the rough voice.

Relief flooded through Rae, setting her rigid, aching muscles to trembling. Grimly, she kept tugging and twisting her wrists, ignoring the pain, the choking fear.

"Lose them," her nemesis ordered without inflection. He wasn't looking at Rae anymore, but she tried to keep her movements to a minimum. If he noticed what she was doing, it would all be over right now.

"They're getting closer!"

"Turn on 30th. Take the road into Garden of the Gods. We'll lose them—and dump her—there."

She had five minutes, maybe less.

She felt blood trickle down; her wrists burned, throbbed; pain shot up into her shoulders as she worked the stiff, stubborn bonds. *Renew my strength, Lord. Mount me on eagle's wings and help me fly away from this danger....*

Caleb, I love you. Where are you?

Huge red monoliths rose in Rae's blurring vision, protruding from the gray-green earth like the dorsal plates on a gigantic stegosaurus. The car swerved into the park entrance on two wheels, throwing Rae across the seat.

"Be careful, you fool!"

The rough words cut across Rae's triumph. Her little finger had slipped free. Her heart jerked once, then tripped over itself when the man turned to stare at her with his lifeless eyes.

"Don't try anything, or I'll break your neck right now."

Rae stared mutely, eyes trapped in his mesmerizing gaze. She shook her head, unable even to swallow. The man turned back around. Rae tugged frantically on the ropes.

Her ring finger slipped past, then her thumb. Tears pouring down her cheeks, she gave one hard tug—and her right hand flopped free, dropping behind her onto the seat like the hand of a—of a corpse.

Sirens keened in the distance, promising help, offering tantalizing hope. But they were still too far away. Too far to help her.

Making sure she kept her hand out of sight behind her back, Rae worked her fingers, praying for feeling, for control of her hand no matter how painful. If she couldn't break free and do something—. She shut her mind to the prospect and prayed.

Prayed for a chance.

"Take that side road—" That was Mr. Dead Voice, sounding urgent now, a lot of the control stripped away. "You can lose them and dump her. What the—!"

Rae attacked like an avenging angel, hurling herself toward the driver. Her hands clawed his face, scratching at his eyes, then flung past to the steering wheel.

She wrenched it as hard as she could.

Hands were grabbing at her; the driver was screaming in her ear, and the world disintegrated into a kaleidoscope of whirling sound and color. The car, swerving like a berserk rocket, crashed through a clump of bushes, spun halfway around, then pitched headfirst down a scrub-choked ravine.

I love you, Caleb. Love you—love—

She drifted back to consciousness slowly, floating like a dying autumn leaf. The roller coaster motion had stopped; the yelling and screaming had stopped. Rae thought she must be dead, because instead of noise and panic and chaos, she could hear Caleb's voice, right next to her ear.

"Rae—" The words were choked, as if he were crying. "Rae,

it's all right. It's over. Rae, I love you. . . ."

She opened her eyes. His face, white and gaunt, rimmed with dust and lines of worry, had never looked more beautiful.

Rae smiled. "What took you so long?"

Caleb stared a minute, then burst out laughing. He hugged her, buried his face in her neck, then lifted his head and covered her face with kisses. "I got here as soon as I could," he murmured against her ear, tenderly mimicking the words he had spoken months earlier—a lifetime ago. "Although my timing wasn't much better than when I was on the second story of the house across the street, is it?"

"Better late than never. . . .Caleb, I love you."

"Hey, Myers, is she all right? The ambulance is on its way." Tray Ramirez slid down the embankment, skidding to a halt next to them.

Rae smiled a beautific, if wobbly, smile. "Believe it or not, I think I'm fine. Nothing that a little more Merthiolate won't heal." She lifted her raw and bloodied wrist, flicking the lock of hair on Caleb's brow with unsteady fingers. "Caleb's pretty good at patching me up; I won't need an ambulance."

She twisted her head, grimaced. "What about—"

Caleb put his hand to her cheek. "I'll tell you all about it later, okay?"

"Everything's cool, Rae," Tray put in. "Don't worry about a thing." He looked down at Caleb. "Take her by the hospital on the way home, hero. You can bring her in tomorrow for the debriefing."

Activity churned all around them. There were lights flashing and radios crackling, voices talking. But Rae looked up into Caleb's eyes, and everything else fell away into a deep indigo twilight.

Instead of a raging sea, she had been transported to still waters. Agent Ramirez was right. Everything else could wait until tomorrow.

"Can we go home now?" she asked, her voice breaking on the last word.

Caleb cupped her face in both hands. "When you're with me and I'm with you—and the Lord's loving hands surround us—we are home." His mouth curved in a smile that made Rae want to curl up and crawl inside it. "God brought us together, love. He might have tested us in the fire awhile, but I think we passed."

His mouth bent and closed over hers, gently, quietly, like a loving benediction. Then he rose, lifting Rae carefully into his arms.

EPILOGUE

They drove to Peterson the next morning, savoring the unaccustomed feeling of safety and peace.

"Y'know, I've learned something about myself," Rae mused as Caleb drove, one arm resting on the open window of the car.

"What did you learn?"

Rae held her bandaged wrists up, examining them in the bright morning sunshine of a perfect spring day. "I learned that I don't have to be in control for things to work out all right." She glanced across at Caleb, smiling a little sheepishly. "All these years. . .I'd been such a wonderful, loving, obedient Christian. I thought I knew all the answers and was grateful for what God had done for me."

They stopped at a traffic light. Caleb looked back at Rae, his eyes caressing. "And then?"

"Then God forced me to face—really face—my past, a present I couldn't control no matter how hard I tried, and a future that, for awhile, didn't even exist."

For a little while there was silence as their thoughts tumbled briefly back to the nightmare of the past twenty-four hours.

"I never realized," Caleb confessed softly, "that the reason I never felt rattled before or—or out-of-control, shall we say—was because I never allowed myself to focus my feelings. I wanted to share the love of Jesus everywhere I went—but not myself."

"Then you met me."

"Yeah. . ." One long arm reached out and tugged a hairpin

free, loosing a tendril. "Then I met you and had about as much control over my feelings as I had over the clouds."

Rae swatted his hand away and tucked her hair back up. "I'm gonna cut it all off," she muttered again under her breath. "Caleb?"

"Yes, love?"

"I'm never going to see my father, am I?"

He hesitated, then answered gently. "Probably not. He's gone to ground again, and might not surface for another five years."

She contemplated her hands and the sore, bandaged wrists another minute. "You know, when Larissa was rubbing my father in my face, so to speak, I felt more. . .more *weariness* than hurt. It's been so many years. . . ."

She dropped her hands back in her lap and smiled a little. "I suppose it still hurts a little—but at least I'm *trying* to let the Lord take over those feelings, instead of handling them myself."

He stretched out one hand and covered hers. They drove the rest of the way in companionable silence.

Admiral Vale's office was crowded. Rae recognized most of the people by now. Tray Ramirez, Det. Grabowski, J.W. and Evan, Agent Hoffman. . .Caleb introduced her to the others—the FBI Denver section chief, the civilian contractor who headed the Starseeker program out at Falcon. . .Admiral Vale.

Overwhelmed and a little intimidated, Rae let the contractor, a nervous, medium-sized man with cowlicks all over his hair, shake her hand until she was afraid he would squeeze it off.

Admiral Vale clapped her shoulder with so much force Caleb had to grab her to keep her from pitching into a wastepaper basket.

"Young lady," he boomed in a clipped, satisfied voice, "The U.S. Space Command, the Air Force—and our country—have a lot to thank you for."

"I didn't do anything," Rae protested. "It was Caleb who

figured it all out."

Everyone grinned.

Rae sat down gingerly in a chair J.W. held for her. Caleb had told her last night that the driver's body had broken her impact and probably saved her life. All she had suffered were some more aches and bruises.

They were all singing an anvil chorus this morning, but she had to know what happened. "Can someone finally tell me the details?" she asked now, her gaze moving shyly over everyone's interested eyes.

"Fill 'er in, Ramirez!" Admiral Vale ordered with a grin. He winked at Rae. "But don't tell anyone a word of what you hear in this room, young woman—or I'll have to have you shot at dawn." He chuckled. "If you're as gung-ho in your faith as Myers here is, I reckon I won't have to worry over the matter."

"We caught Fisher at the airport—he's agreed to turn state's evidence," Tray began. "Larissa Holman, the woman who engineered the attempted murder, was his contact with IOS. She used a combination of blackmail, flattery, and the promise of money to lure him."

Rae shuddered at the memory of the woman. "A black widow spider," she observed, earning quick grins from all the men. "Did you catch her?"

Ramirez hesitated, glanced at Caleb. Caleb nodded. His hip rested on the table next to Rae, and he reached a hand down to hers.

"She's dead," Tray said flatly. "Her car spun out of control in a high-speed chase down the freeway—she was doing well over a hundred. Didn't stand a chance in that Corvette." He paused. "She tried to exit where there wasn't one. Car flipped six times."

He glanced away from Rae, staring soberly down at the table. "It crumpled like a squashed bug. . .and Holman wasn't wearing a seatbelt."

"The worst part of it is that means a dead end to tracking

down IOS," Hoffman muttered, rather callously, Rae thought.

She closed her eyes and leaned against Caleb. "What about the other two men?" she asked after a minute.

"They won't be going anywhere for awhile," Det. Grabowski assured her with satisfaction. "The one called Romo has a broken collarbone and a concussion. Jules broke both legs and a couple of ribs. But they'll be well by the time we bring 'em to trial for attempted murder. Among other things."

"Were they from IOS?"

"Probably," Tray Ramirez took up the narrative again. "Neither one of them is talking right now. We'll find out, though."

Agent Hoffman slid a piece of sheet music across the table. "You might be interested in that," he said when she looked at him with questioning eyes.

Rae saw that it was the Mendelssohn. She opened it, and saw a single sheet of paper on top of the music. "Your time has run out," it read. "We require the rest of the program within 72 hours. Otherwise, no additional funds will be deposited in your account. KOLAZO"

"That's what sent Fisher over the edge," Caleb nodded at the note, answering the confusion in Rae's eyes when no one else said anything. "He'd been passing the Starseeker program a few lines at a time, remember?"

Rae nodded.

"IOS apparently got impatient. Larissa sensed everything closing in, and she leaned on Fisher. When he came in Joyful Noise the other day, and you were so nervous, he was petrified that everything was about to go up in smoke.'

"Everything did," Ramirez commented with satisfaction. "Thanks to the courage of a woman who took a lot of abuse from a lot of different sources the past few months."

Rae shrugged, coloring. "You had cause. . . ." Now that it was all over, it was easier to be magnanimous.

"Did anyone ever figure out what *kolazo* meant?" Agent Hoffman asked. "All I know is that it's Greek."

"I looked it up in a copy of *Vine's Expository Dictionary* last night," Caleb informed the astonished audience. "Rae had one in her uncle's old library, buried under a pile of music and dust."

Rae elbowed his ribs.

"I think that one word's the reason Fisher panicked, more than the body of the note. According to the book, it denotes punishment—vengeance. I think IOS was telling him something."

Admiral Vale shook his head. "You're something else, son. Anytime you want to quit messing around the Defense Security Agency, let me know. The Navy could use a few good men, too."

Rae looked up at Agent Ramirez. "What about my father?" she asked, not quite able to disguise the weariness and shame. "Caleb said he's gone to ground again." She bit her lip. "I'm sorry about all the trouble he's caused."

"Miss Prescott, we're the ones who are sorry for having to treat you as a suspect—because of him."

"Rae. . ." Caleb turned and knelt in front of her, taking her hands. "Remember? You're not responsible for the sins of your father." His thumbs traced a tender caressing path over her knuckles. "There is another way to look at this, too, you know."

He waited until Rae nodded. "You and I have acknowledged that God has been and always will be in perfect control; now we can also accept a lesson about His perfect timing. He brought us together, using your father, don't you see? You probably wouldn't have been involved in the case if your father hadn't pulled you in, however circumspectly."

Caleb and Rae ignored the others. "I do have a solution, though, if you have a problem with the Prescott name," Caleb murmured, his eyes locked with hers. "You could change it—to Myers."

Rae blushed crimson, but her eyes glowed. "I think I could

191

learn to live with that name with no trouble at all," she admitted.

Caleb drew her up, and laughter and good-natured heckling filled the room like effervescent bubbles. Someone produced Styrofoam cups and a couple of cans of soft drinks. Amid congratulations, hugs, and teasing kisses, Rae toasted her new fiance—and spilled half the drink in her lap.

"We'll have to have *Ode to Joy* as our processional," she announced after mopping off her skirt with resigned good humor.

"You mean the one from Beethoven's Fifth?" Caleb asked with a mischievous grin.

"I thought the *Ode to Joy* was from Beethoven's Ninth," Admiral Vale commented with perplexity.

Fresh laughter erupted from everyone, and Rae threw her arms around Caleb. "Who cares?" She smiled at the circle of indulgent masculine faces. "We'll have them both!"